John Creasey

Born in Surrey, England in 19(were nine children, John Creasey grew up to be a true master story teller and international sensation. His more than 600 crime, mystery and thriller titles have now sold 80 million copies in 25 languages. These include many popular series such as *Gideon of Scotland Yard*, *The Toff*, *Dr Palfrey* and *The Baron*.

Creasy wrote under many pseudonyms, explaining that booksellers had complained he totally dominated the 'C' section in stores. They included:

Gordon Ashe, M E Cooke, Norman Deane, Robert Caine Frazer, Patrick Gill, Michael Halliday, Charles Hogarth, Brian Hope, Colin Hughes, Kyle Hunt, Abel Mann, Peter Manton, J J Marric, Richard Martin, Rodney Mattheson, Anthony Morton and *Jeremy York*.

Never one to sit still, Creasey had a strong social conscience, and stood for Parliament several times, along with founding the One Party Alliance which promoted the idea of government by a coalition of the best minds from across the political spectrum.

He also founded the British Crime Writers' Association, which to this day celebrates outstanding crime writing. The Mystery Writers of America bestowed upon him the Edgar Award for best novel and then in 1969 the ultimate Grand Master Award. John Creasey's stories are as compelling today as ever.

INPECTOR WEST SERIES

INSPECTOR WEST TAKES CHARGE
INSPECTOR WEST LEAVES TOWN (ALSO PUBLISHED AS: GO AWAY TO MURDER)
INSPECTOR WEST AT HOME (ALSO PUBLISHED AS: AN APOSTLE OF GLOOM)
INSPECTOR WEST REGRETS
HOLIDAY FOR INSPECTOR WEST
BATTLE FOR INSPECTOR WEST
TRIUMPH FOR INSPECTOR WEST (ALSO PUBLISHED AS: THE CASE AGAINST PAUL RAEBURN)
INSPECTOR WEST KICKS OFF (ALSO PUBLISHED AS: SPORT FOR INSPECTOR WEST)
INSPECTOR WEST ALONE
INSPECTOR WEST CRIES WOLF (ALSO PUBLISHED AS: THE CREEPERS)
A CASE FOR INSPECTOR WEST (ALSO PUBLISHED AS: THE FIGURE IN THE DUSK)
PUZZLE FOR INSPECTOR WEST (ALSO PUBLISHED AS: THE DISSEMBLERS)
INSPECTOR WEST AT BAY (ALSO PUBLISHED AS: THE CASE OF THE ACID THROWERS)
A GUN FOR INSPECTOR WEST (ALSO PUBLISHED AS: GIVE A MAN A GUN)
SEND INSPECTOR WEST (ALSO PUBLISHED AS: SEND SUPERINTENDENT WEST)
A BEAUTY FOR INSPECTOR WEST (ALSO PUBLISHED AS: THE BEAUTY QUEEN KILLER)
INSPECTOR WEST MAKES HASTE (ALSO PUBLISHED AS: MURDER MAKES HASTE)
TWO FOR INSPECTOR WEST (ALSO PUBLISHED AS: MURDER: ONE, TWO, THREE)
PARCELS FOR INSPECTOR WEST (ALSO PUBLISHED AS: DEATH OF A POSTMAN)
A PRINCE FOR INSPECTOR WEST (ALSO PUBLISHED AS: DEATH OF A ASSASSIN)
ACCIDENT FOR INSPECTOR WEST (ALSO PUBLISHED AS: HIT AND RUN)
FIND INSPECTOR WEST (ALSO PUBLISHED AS: DOORWAY TO DEATH)
MURDER, LONDON - NEW YORK
STRIKE FOR DEATH (ALSO PUBLISHED AS: THE KILLING STRIKE)
DEATH OF A RACEHORSE
THE CASE OF THE INNOCENT VICTIMS
MURDER ON THE LINE
DEATH IN COLD PRINT
THE SCENE OF THE CRIME
POLICEMAN'S DREAD
HANG THE LITTLE MAN
LOOK THREE WAYS AT MURDER
MURDER, LONDON - AUSTRALIA
MURDER, LONDON - SOUTH AFRICA
THE EXECUTIONERS
SO YOUNG TO BURN
MURDER, LONDON - MIAMI
A PART FOR A POLICEMAN
ALIBI (ALSO PUBLISHED AS: ALIBI FOR INSPECTOR WEST)
A SPLINTER OF GLASS
THE THEFT OF MAGNA CARTA
THE EXTORTIONERS
A SHARP RISE IN CRIME

Doorway To Death

(Find Inspector West,

The Trouble at Saxby's)

John Creasey

Copyright © 1957 John Creasey Literary Management Ltd.
© 2014 House of Stratus

All rights reserved. No part of this publication may be reproduced, stored in a retrieval system, or transmitted, in any form, or by any means (electronic, mechanical, photocopying, recording, or otherwise), without the prior permission of the publisher. Any person who does any unauthorised act in relation to this publication may be liable to criminal prosecution and civil claims for damages.

The right of John Creasey to be identified as the author of this work has been asserted.

This edition published in 2014 by House of Stratus, an imprint of Stratus Books Ltd., Lisandra House, Fore Street, Looe, Cornwall, PL13 1AD, U.K.
www.houseofstratus.com

Typeset by House of Stratus.

A catalogue record for this book is available from the British Library and the Library of Congress.

ISBN 07551-3675-6
EAN 978-07551-3675-9

This book is sold subject to the condition that it shall not be lent, resold, hired out, or otherwise circulated without the publisher's express prior consent in any form of binding, or cover, other than the original as herein published and without a similar condition being imposed on any subsequent purchaser, or bona fide possessor.

This is a fictional work and all characters are drawn from the author's imagination. Any resemblance or similarities to persons either living or dead are entirely coincidental.

PROLOGUE

Michael Quist studied the cheques very closely through a magnifying glass, and then put the last one down on the desk in his small office. It had been altered cleverly, from one hundred and seventy-five pounds to nine hundred and seventy-five.

He had spent the day checking payments against invoices, and found some other small mistakes, but all of those could be put down to error.

There was no question of error with the last one. It was in favour of Thomas Cole and Company, and passed and endorsed on the back by T. Cole. Undoubtedly three other cheques, each made out to a different small firm, had also been tampered with; he had found these after scrutinising every cancelled cheque that seemed even slightly suspect.

There might be others.

The remarkable thing was that each altered cheque had been passed by the bank, although he had spotted the alteration quickly. Anyone who specialised in scrutinising cheques should have queried it.

No one had.

But the bank cashier who had scrawled his initials over these, in approval, was a certain Charles Henry, who worked closely with Saxby's; and Henry was usually eagle-eyed in scrutiny.

How was it he had passed these?

Normally, Quist would have taken the cheque to the secretary, but the great man was away in America for the next two months. Gorringe, the second-in-command and now in charge, would doubtless applaud his junior's acute observation, and arrange things so that he, Gorringe, and not a comparative newcomer to the accountancy staff, took the credit.

"And that would be a pity," Quist mused, still tense with the excitement of his discovery. "I think I'll probe a bit myself."

The first essential thing was to have a look at other cheques drawn in favour of the same firms, to get access to the bank statements without arousing anyone's curiosity, and try to have a complete survey ready by the time the great man returned. He must watch future cheques closely, too. If any newly-drawn ones were altered, he would have to report to Gorringe at once; the damage was already done with these, so delay should do no harm. The more he discovered for himself, the more difficult it would be for Gorringe to usurp the credit.

To Quist, this was a heaven-sent opportunity to prove his value to Saxby's. He set about the task carefully, but at once, and it was not long before his suspicions of Charles Henry, the bank cashier, grew stronger.

Chapter One

Fear

Charles Henry was dozing when the telephone rang. It startled him, as it always did these days, and he sat bolt upright in his armchair. His back was to the window, the lawn, the flowers and the evening sun. From the garden there was the sound of a hedge being clipped.

Henry placed his large hands on the arm of his chair, and heaved himself to his feet. He was big and overweight, and the movement was an effort. He looked round swiftly, almost furtively, but the clipping continued uninterrupted, a kind of peaceful reminder of living. There was no other sound, until the telephone blared out again.

It was in the hall of this small, suburban house.

Henry ran his hands over his balding head, and moved towards the door, still physically powerful although well past his peak, for he was in his sixties. He was wearing grey flannels and an open-necked shirt, and the trousers were unbuttoned at the waist. He did the buttons up as he reached the hall, snatched up the telephone, and cut the ringing short.

"Hallo?"

A man said: "Who is that?"

"This—this is Charles Henry speaking." Henry clenched the telephone tightly, and looked about him, up the flight of narrow stairs to the landing, then towards the front door, which stood ajar, letting the bright light in.

The man at the other end of the telephone said: "There'll be another one tomorrow," in a flat voice.

"No!" ejaculated Henry. "No, I can't! It's impossible so soon!"

"Tomorrow, and don't forget," the man said, and rang off.

Henry did not put the receiver down immediately, but stood looking at the partly open door, which swayed gently in the evening breeze. His breathing was short and laboured, his jaw and lips were set, and a film of sweat which had not been there before was on his forehead. Slowly, he put the receiver down, and as he did so new and different sounds came in. Footsteps in the garden, a girl calling: "Hallo, Mike," and then more footsteps, undoubtedly Sybil hurrying to greet her new boy friend, eager for a quick kiss, a hug, a smile. They were a few yards away, and yet might have been a thousand miles from here for all the help they were to Charles Henry.

The footsteps stopped; they were kissing. Henry could not see them, but he knew.

"Oh, God," he breathed.

Then he heard another sound, and turned his head swiftly, almost as if in fear. He stood gaping towards the head of the stairs.

His wife stood there.

She was looking at him in a way which had become almost normal in the past few months, as if in despair; as if her love for him was kept at bay by the barrier which had come between them. She had always been the lover and he the beloved, but the years had brought them together so closely that until recently they thought and talked and worked and played as if of one mind.

A few months ago all that had ended.

"Charles," his wife began, and stopped.

Henry didn't answer.

"Charles, why don't you tell me what it is? Why do you keep it to yourself?" Grace Henry began to move towards him, one stair at a time, her small, pale hands tight on the banister rail, her voice carrying not only to the hall but outside, where Sybil and her Michael were still silent.

To the wife, also, these two might have been a thousand miles away; all she could see and think of was her husband.

"Charles, I can't stand it any longer. You look—you look like death."

He didn't speak.

She reached the bottom stair.

"Charles, you must tell me what it is," Mrs. Henry persisted in that low-pitched yet carrying voice. "I can't stand the strain any longer, I really can't. Is—is it something at the bank? Have you embezzled some money?" When her husband didn't answer, just stared as if unseeing, she became shrill in desperation: "I don't care what it is, I don't care how bad it is, but I must *know*. I can't help unless I know. Charles, in God's name, tell me what it is."

"You help, Grace," he said, in a voice as tense as hers, but hoarse and uneven. "You help by—by just being yourself. It—it won't be much longer. Then—then perhaps I'll be able to tell you about it. But it will soon be over, I—I'm sure. Don't worry me now."

"That's what you always say," Grace protested, still shrill and insistent. "You've been saying exactly the same thing for weeks—for months! It's no use, I've got to know." She moved towards him and clasped his big, soft hands. "Charles, can't you see that? I'll do anything I can to help. I don't care what you've done, but we can't go on like this any longer."

Henry moistened his lips. The pale flesh sagged beneath his chin, there were pouches beneath his eyes, and a kind of frightening helplessness. He freed his right hand, patted hers in a futile gesture, then moved away.

"I'm sorry, Grace. I have to go out for an hour or two this evening. I won't be any later than I can help."

"Charles," said his wife, now in a low-pitched, determined voice, "you're not going out tonight and you're not going anywhere again until you tell me what is affecting you like this."

"Now, now, Grace, please."

"I can't put off any longer, I must know."

"Grace, please."

"You're not going out of this house until—" Mrs. Henry began. But abruptly she broke off, because of the change in her husband's expression. She saw him as she had never really seen him before, in anger which put fire into his eyes, roughness in his voice, and brutal strength into his hand as he gripped her wrist.

"Don't keep nagging me! I'm going out. I'll go where I like and when I like, and I won't have any interference from you or anyone. Is that clear?"

She was shocked into silence.

He shouted: "Is that clear?"

"It—yes," mumbled Grace, all determination gone. "Yes, Charles, I—I only want to help you."

"The way to help me is to stop nagging, and pestering me with questions," Charles Henry said. "Let's understand that once and for all."

He pushed past his wife and started up the stairs, without looking back even at the landing. Grace Henry turned and watched him. Tears shimmered in her grey eyes, but did not fall. She was a tall, slim woman, who had kept her figure remarkably in middle-age, but whose hair was iron grey and whose face was beginning to show lines which betrayed her years. She wore a dark blue linen dress, trimmed with white, and with a wide white belt; but its youthfulness was lost on her.

Her husband went into the bedroom, and the door closed.

Outside, in the garden, Sybil Henry had heard the telephone ringing, and at first had not given it a serious thought. She had known that both her mother and her father were indoors, so one or the other would answer it. It held no terrors for her, aroused no fears. She knew that her father wasn't well, and was worried because that seemed to distress her mother, but the anxiety did not go deep. If challenged, she would have denied the reason for this: that her affection for her father did not go very deep, either. He was part of the background of life, but these days he did not affect her life very much, for she was at home only at weekends and occasionally on holiday.

She had been trimming a low hedge of box privet, an easy job, and kept glancing round towards the street and the corner, hoping that it would not be long before Michael came. When she first saw him, he was cycling; she went on clipping, deliberately, anxious not to give away the fact that all her inclination was to fling down the shears and rush towards him. He stood the bicycle against the kerb, and came into the garden, tall, brisk, lithe. He wasn't exactly dashingly handsome, but it was easy to forget that, especially when laughter seemed to spring from his eyes.

He didn't speak, and in a way seemed to imply that he knew what she was feeling; for there he was, smiling, inviting her to hurry to him, almost drawing her near by a kind of magnetism. And she could not help herself; she actually ran the last few steps, and he looked eager and delighted as he first hugged and then kissed her. The things they said didn't matter.

"Hallo, Sybil. Am I late?"

"Hardly."

"Sorry."

"It doesn't matter."

"It's criminal. That's a nice hedge."

"Is it?"

"Magnificently trimmed."

"My mother does it once a week."

He grinned. "Liar."

All this time they had been standing very close to each other, looking into each other's eyes. Two or three neighbours were in sight, in nearby gardens, but the couple were oblivious of this, as of the house. Except for the soft breeze, the evening was warm, the sun touched the tops of the trees which grew along the winding street, caught the coloured tiles of the roofs and, where hedges were low, the flowers in beds and in borders. The world of Laurel Avenue was of colour and brightness.

This was really the first time that Sybil had been quite sure how she felt about Michael Quist. She had known that she liked the way he looked, smiled, moved and walked; how he kissed, yet did not presume that she wanted only caresses. He had interested her since they had first met, a few weeks ago, and tonight she had looked forward very much to his coming. The moment when she had first seen him her heart had leapt, telling its tale. Then he had virtually willed her to hurry towards him. Now her heart was beating fast and she could still feel the pressure of his firm body and of his lips in the kiss of greeting. He was no longer smiling in that rather bold, gay way; there was the tension in him, as of a new discovery.

"Sybil," he said, rather abruptly.

"Yes?"

"There's something I particularly want to tell you. Can you come out for an hour or so?"

"Yes."

"Need a coat?"

"I'll get my handbag, and tell mother," Sybil said.

"Right."

She turned towards the front door, which stood ajar. They had heard nothing of her father speaking on the telephone, for they had been in that other world.

Now Quist saw Sybil turn away from him, and her swift, graceful movement made him catch his breath. She wasn't really small, and she had – everything. The sun's rays caught the side of her face, with its smooth, clear, creamy skin, her fine hair, drawn rather lightly back from her forehead, her little, snug ear. She was wearing a green cotton dress, and he did not realise how subtly it emphasised her figure. Her legs and ankles were beautiful.

Then he heard a woman say, as if angrily: "Charles!"

Sybil missed a step, startled, and didn't go on. There was a long silence, before the woman, her mother, went on to say in a voice which Quist hardly recognised: "Charles, why don't you tell me what it is? Why do you keep it to yourself?"

The way Sybil turned to look at Quist, as if hating the fact that he heard, seemed to give added significance to the words. There were more, which he didn't hear clearly because a motor-cycle passed along the street, its engine noisy and offensive. Sybil didn't go any nearer the house, and Quist moved towards her, putting an arm firmly round her waist. They stood quite still, looking at the open door, hearing everything now but seeing nothing. Sybil seemed to hold herself very taut. Quist glanced down and saw the tension at her lips, the way her hands were clenched.

Then Charles Henry shouted. The rage was all too evident; he sounded as if he hated his wife.

"Is that clear?" he bellowed.

Grace Henry said something in a voice pitched so low that Sybil and Quist couldn't hear what it was. There were movements, as of footsteps, but Sybil didn't move. Quist's hand was at her waist, and he squeezed gently, trying to give her some comfort. She stared at the doorway, and said: "I'm sorry."

"There's no need to be."

"I must go and see mother."

"Yes, of course."

She looked up at him, her eyes very bright.

"Mick, you do understand, don't you?"

"I understand perfectly," Quist said. "You may be needed here. I gather that they don't—" He broke off.

"What?"

"Quarrel often?"

"Hardly ever, until lately."

"No need to go on," Quist said gruffly. "It's none of my business. There's just one thing."

Her eyes asked him what that was.

"If there's any way I can help, let me know."

"I don't think there is, but I'll tell you," Sybil said, and suddenly took his hands. "Mick, please don't go away yet. Why—why don't you clip the hedge for five minutes? This may fizzle out, and I may be able to come."

"I'll stay," Quist promised, and stood and watched as she hurried to the porch, opened the door and stepped into the house. Then he went towards the small shears she had been using, bent down, and picked them up. Doing so, he caught a glimpse of movement out of the corner of his eyes, and saw Sybil's father standing at a top-floor window.

It was like looking upon fear.

Quist felt sure that he knew the cause of that fear.

He had wanted to tell Sybil the truth, long before this had happened. That he, Michael Quist, had been spying on her father.

That he believed Henry to be party to a serious crime. That he had schemed an introduction to her so as to get to know her father, and had fallen in love with her.

Soon she was going to be hurt. If she learned about his part in it, she would be hurt even more.

If she loved him.

Chapter Two

Meeting

It was twenty minutes before Sybil came out again, and in that time Quist had clipped about two square feet of hedge, and spent much of the time day-dreaming. But the exaltation he had felt when he had asked Sybil to come out for an hour or two had faded completely. There had been magic, and the magic was gone; he had the sense to know that he couldn't command it to come back. He also had the sense to know that something quite exceptional had happened to him when his heart lurched, almost painfully, at sight of Sybil coming out of the side door of the house. She moved with such easy grace, very light on her feet; but her expression told him that there had been no easing of the tension indoors. As she came out of the shadow of the house into the sunlight of the garden, he saw a vivid likeness between her and her father, in spite of her father's full, fleshy face; and in spite of his fear.

Sybil had startlingly blue eyes.

Quist smiled, and held out the shears.

"All right, I surrender," he said. "I'll come again tomorrow, and hope things are better."

"Mick," she asked, "will you do something for me?"

That was quite unexpected, and he showed his surprise, but said quickly: "Yes, of course," and waited for her to explain.

She hesitated, glancing away from him towards the road where people walked by, and then back at him, as if she wasn't happy about the request she had to make.

"There's no reason why you should," she said rather quickly. "It isn't your affair, and—well, we hardly know each other, do we? If you'd rather not do it, please say so."

"I want to help if I can." God knew he did.

"I mean, if you'd rather not do this particular thing." Sybil hesitated, and looked quickly over her shoulder, as if afraid that they were being watched. Then she took Michael's hand and led him further away from the house, as if to make sure that they weren't overheard. "Mick, it's a long story really, and I can't explain because I don't know what's behind it, but about two or three months ago my father—my father started to act a little oddly."

Quist just said: "Mm-mm," non-committally.

"Mother hardly noticed it at first," Sybil went on. "Father was home a little later some evenings, and occasionally he would go out without telling her where he was going. Trivial things like that. It—it was especially strange because he's always been a creature of habit. You know that he works at Southern National Bank, don't you?"

"You told me." As if he hadn't known before he'd met her! "He's head cashier at the Hadworth branch."

"Yes, he—but that doesn't matter. The important thing is that he began to worry mother," Sybil went on quickly, and it would not take much to make her wish that she hadn't started to talk. It behoved Michael Quist to be very careful what he said and how he looked; it would be easy to make her stop, and so cause embarrassment which would give them a new problem of their own. "Once or twice most weeks he has a telephone call in the evening. Sometimes he shuts himself in his room upstairs after it, sometimes he goes out. When he goes out, he's usually gone two hours or so. Mother has no idea where he goes or what he does. At first he pretended that he was going to see a friend, but lately he's given up pretending. She keeps trying to make him explain, but he won't, and—well she's frightened by it now. And I could kick myself."

"What have you done?"

"That's the trouble. I've done nothing."

"Didn't you know what was going on?"

"Well, I suppose I did," Sybil said slowly. "Mother told me that something was worrying him, and he's certainly looked ill. I suppose the truth is that I didn't take it very seriously, even when I was home. Mother didn't tell me how unhappy it was making her, and I can see now that she was anxious not to worry me. I should have realised it, but I've been so busy with my own silly affairs—" Sybil was a little flushed, and the colour in her cheeks and the glint in her eyes made Quist wish he could stand and look at her for a long time.

At least she was finding it easier to talk.

"I can't alter what's been done," she said, still vexedly, "but I can try to help now. I wonder if you would try to find out where—"

She broke off, as if only then did she realise what she was asking. She looked away from him quickly, as if she was anxious not to see his expression.

"Mick, I'm sorry; you can't possibly. Forget it. I'll give you a ring tomorrow."

"Don't be silly," Quist said quickly. "There's no reason at all why I shouldn't try to find out where he goes, if you really want me to. Er—there's one thing you might have overlooked, though. I don't want to drop a brick, but you know the obvious explanation, don't you?"

"Oh, yes; another woman," said Sybil, almost offhandedly. "I hate even to think that's it."

She brightened up a lot when Quist insisted on trying to help; but if her father was involved with another woman, she and her mother would be in for a nasty time. And if Sybil then found out why Quist had come to know her—

Her hand on his was light but firm. Trusting.

"Sure you don't mind, Mick?"

"I'm positive," he said. "But don't blame me if you wish you'd never heard of me when I've reported." He sounded almost grim.

"Mick, don't be silly! I've been talking to mother, and she says she knows that father often catches a bus at the end of the road and gets off at Hadworth Station. She doesn't know what he does then. If you—"

Quist took her by the shoulders, kissed her firmly and then dropped his arms and turned and walked off. She watched every step, until he turned from the gate to wave.

Sybil saw Michael glance up at the upper windows, and then sit astride his bicycle and pedal off. He didn't look back again, and she was glad, for there were tears in her eyes, and she saw him through a haze.

Why had this thing happened now, of all times?

She felt a great bitterness towards her father because he had spoiled the magic of the evening. No matter how understanding Michael was, he could not fail to be affected by this dismal family trouble. She wished that she hadn't asked him to spy on her father, and could well believe that she had only made the situation worse. It was hard to understand the expression in Mike's eyes when he had agreed to go; hard to understand why he had said that she might wish she'd never heard of him.

It was almost as if he knew something already.

Nonsense!

Her mother came to the window and looked out, but did not speak or beckon. Then Sybil heard footsteps. Her father appeared at the front door, carrying a bowler hat and an umbrella, looking as respectable as a man could; a tower of strength, a regular pillar of society, she thought bitterly. She saw the way her mother was looking at him, and realised what awful hurt he had caused her; that turned bitterness almost into hatred.

Then she saw her father's face.

Bitterness and hatred faded in deep compassion. It was easy to see how much he suffered, too. Some cruel thing was tormenting him, and suddenly she wanted to help, to do something, anything, to ease the burden.

She hurried towards him, hands outstretched.

"Dad, is there anything at all that I can do?"

"Go to your mother," he said in a harsh, commanding voice.

She drew back, dropping her hand, coldness quickly replacing the warmth of compassion. That was how it had always been; he had managed to stifle her affection.

Her mother had seen her gesture, and the rebuff.

Sybil went in to her, wishing more than ever that she had not asked Michael to go.

What *had* he meant?

She heard a motor-cycle start up.

That was not unusual, for in Laurel Avenue there were a dozen youths with motor-cycles or Vespas, the staccato noise of engines was a part of the background noise of the neighbourhood. Sybil did not even glance towards it; it did not occur to her that her father was being followed, and that Michael would be noticed, too.

Her thoughts were mostly on Michael. How hard he worked, how much he studied in the evening, how he had snatched precious hours for tonight, how he preferred a bicycle to a car, because the car would tempt him out into the country too often.

"There'll be plenty of time for that later," he had told her, half laughingly.

That reminded her how little she really knew about him. An acquaintance had introduced them only three weeks ago, at North Hadworth Tennis Club, the day he had joined. She knew that he worked at Saxby's, a manufacturing company with its works on the outskirts of the London suburb. He was in the secretary's office in the West End, training for some kind of job which he hadn't talked much about. He had a small flat in Hadworth, near the station, and spent part of his time at the factory, part at the West End office.

That was really all she knew.

Except that she was desperately in love with him, and although she had tried not to admit it, had been from the first time she had seen him. Love at first sight had seemed too absurd, so school-girlish, but there it was.

She would have to stop thinking about Michael now, and hope desperately that this would not make any difference to the way he thought of her. Even while she was talking to her mother and trying to comfort her, that thought was uppermost in her mind.

As Michael Quist reached the end of the avenue, a man on a motor-cycle, at the side of the road, glanced at him but showed no sign of deep interest. But after he had reached the main road, the motor-cyclist followed, and watched him as he rode down the hill towards the station. A few minutes later, Charles Henry appeared, and boarded a bus going in the same direction as Quist.

The motor-cyclist went ahead of the bus, and reached Hadworth Hill station a few seconds before Quist, who saw the man without really noticing him.

The bus came up.

Henry got off, heavily, and made straight for one of the several taxis waiting nearby. The motor-cyclist watched Quist, who sat astride his bicycle on the other side of the wide road.

Obviously he had to choose between trying to keep up with the taxi on the bicycle, or hurrying across the road, hiring another cab and asking the driver to keep the first in sight. In the moment of indecision, another crowd came from the station and two men hurried for taxis. The one which Henry had hired was already moving away, and Quist cycled off first, going very fast down a short, steep hill. By day, his task would have been easy, for traffic would have slowed the taxi down; but there was little about now, and the High Street stretched wide and almost empty. The motor-cyclist, following, saw him shoot past a set of traffic lights as they changed from amber to red; the taxi was held up. Quist's next problem would be whether to turn right at the second lights or go straight on, towards London. If he waited, he would lose the taxi anyhow, so went straight on.

The taxi followed, with the motor-cyclist a little way behind.

Now it was a kind of game, and a cyclist's only hope of keeping the taxi in sight was to keep ahead or catch up with it at traffic lights. One after another these turned red, and helped Quist, who kept looking round. The taxi took a corner behind him, and he braked fiercely, made a U turn, and cycled furiously back.

The motor-cyclist grinned.

The taxi was out of sight of them both.

There was a warren of streets here, some at right angles, some at acute angles to others; there were small *cul-de-sacs*, too, a dozen places where the taxi might go. Quist sped on, glancing right and left into turnings and narrow streets with small, terraced houses on either side, all looking very much alike. Most had a bush or two outside in a tiny garden. The road surface was of loose gravel, for it had been freshly tarred, and the warmth of the evening made the smell stick in his throat.

Then, the taxi came out of a street, its *For Hire* sign up, and along the same street, Charles Henry was going into a public-house.

Quist didn't know whether to be disappointed or not. He cycled along, and saw that the pub was the Rose and Crown, and that the door Henry had entered by was marked *"Saloon Bar"*. Quist went into the Lounge Bar, and ordered a beer; he could just see Henry in the next room.

Henry soon moved out of sight.

Quist downed his beer, hurried into the street, and saw Henry already turning a corner. Quist got on to his bicycle, and tried not to show how much he hurried.

Henry was fumbling at the letter-box of a house a little way along. He pulled something out – obviously a key dangling on a piece of string inside the door. Henry let himself in, and pushed the key back again.

Quist cycled past.

Two minutes later he turned back. He noticed a motorcyclist at one end of the street, but took no notice of him. At the window of a room upstairs was a woman whom he saw quite clearly; fine, bold, handsome.

Then he saw Henry join her.

It was ten o'clock before Quist got back to Laurel Avenue, and even then he was ahead of Charles Henry, Sybil saw him turning in at the gate. Her mother had gone into a neighbour's to help with a sick child, jumping at the chance to take her mind off her worry. For nearly an hour Sybil had been alone.

She hurried to the door as Quist came up the path. The light from the porch and the hall shone on his face, and she searched it for news. It was set hard, relaxing into a smile only when he saw her.

"Darling, ever since you left I've been hating myself for asking you to go. I'm so sorry that—"

"You don't have to be sorry," Quist said, and took her by the shoulders. His eyes seemed to be searching hers intently. "Sybil, you want the truth, don't you?"

"Of course I do."

"Where's your mother?"

"She's out, it's all right. Mike, was it—was it another woman?"

"Yes." Obviously he hated telling her, and his grip was harder. "It was a woman of about forty, quite presentable, rather big and handsome. I saw him go into her house and saw them together at a window upstairs. I hate saying it, darling, but you must be prepared for—for a lot of unpleasantness."

Sybil didn't speak. Of course her mother suspected the truth, but when she heard of this—

"I shouldn't have told you," Quist said, almost roughly. "I ought to have said that I couldn't find anything out, but lying would only hurt more."

"Of course you had to tell me," Sybil said, rather wearily. "I suppose she's got him under her thumb, and he can't get away. I wish I knew how to help him."

"Listen, sweetheart," Michael said, "don't even *try*. It wouldn't be any use interfering, this is a thing he has to work out for himself. Your job is to help your mother, that's all. Don't you go following your father, or trying to find this woman. It would only make things worse."

He was almost fierce in his insistence.

"It's all right," Sybil assured him. "I won't be so silly as that. I just wish it hadn't happened. What *was* she like? Really attractive?"

"Well, I only had a glimpse of her," Quist admitted, as if grudgingly. "You know Lorna Morne, at the club?"

"Yes."

"Not unlike her."

Sybil had a mental picture of a woman in her late thirties, dark-haired, with a fine, full-breasted figure and a small waist; a rather handsome, colourful, sexy type, as different from her mother as anyone could be. Somehow it was easier to understand; and somehow she felt even more grateful to Michael.

"Listen, Sybil," he said abruptly. "I couldn't help hurting you. Whatever happens, remember that."

"Of course I'll remember," Sybil promised.

His manner puzzled her, and she wanted to ask him what he meant by 'whatever happens', but she heard her mother coming back. She was glad that Michael decided to go then, and slipped out by the side door.

About eleven o'clock her father came home, and went straight up to the bedroom. Sybil caught a glimpse of him on the landing, and was surprised to see that he looked almost cheerful. A little later she heard him talking quite amiably to her mother. He'd had a drink or two, of course, but sometimes drink made him morose.

Could he have freed himself from that unknown woman?

Certainly there seemed no reason why Michael should have been so worried.

It was lunch-time next day when Sybil, sitting on a bench in St. James's Park with her sandwiches, saw a photograph of her father's mistress. It was the word 'murder' which caught her eye, and she found herself leading over the shoulder in an evening paper of a woman who must be rather like of the man with the newspaper.

There was a bold headline, followed by a short paragraph which seemed almost as if it was there for her to read.

WOMAN MURDERED IN BED
Scotland Yard officers are anxious to interview a cyclist known to have been in Page Street, Elwell, at about nine o'clock last night, and who is believed to have cycled away in the direction of Hadworth. Anyone in the Hadworth or Elwell district who saw a cyclist riding

a new-looking, pale green machine, wearing grey flannel trousers, a brown sports jacket, and without a hat, is asked to communicate with Chief Inspector West of New Scotland Yard immediately.

It was absurd, of course; the woman reminded her of Lorna Morne, and the description fitted Michael.

She must forget it.

Chapter Three

Work For West

Chief Inspector Roger West of New Scotland Yard turned over the several photographs of the dead woman, some of them taken in life and found at her flat, some of them taken after death. No art studio could have done these better. West put three of them aside, and as he did so, the Chief Inspector sitting at the next desk looked across and grinned.

"Feeling sorry you didn't know her before she died?"

West kept a straight face.

"If I had I'd know her friends, and probably the one who did this," he said.

The C.I. grimaced. "Handsome West, always on the ball! I ought to have known. Got anything yet?"

"Only this cyclist," said West. "I don't know how much notice to take of that yet." He tapped a small sheaf of papers on his desk, all reports from the detectives who had been working in Page Street, Elwell, since the discovery of the murder, at seven o'clock that morning. "It's nearly always the same: neighbours go deaf, dumb and blind when you want anything on a murder job. Only three admit noticing anyone. Two, including a woman in the downstairs flat at the house, saw the cyclist. One says she also saw a fattish, elderly man go into the house. One of the Divisional coppers saw the cyclist, but doesn't mention the fattish chap. Sooner we talk to the copper the better."

"Know anything about the dead woman?" The other C.I. was looking at the photographs.

"Her name was Rose Jensen, known as Miss, but there are one or two small callouses on the wedding-ring finger. She'd worn a ring there for a long time. She moved to Page Street in the winter, January or February, taking the upstairs flat. It's self-contained. Haven't found out where she worked. She kept herself to herself, as the neighbours say, and they didn't want it any other way. As it was, some said they didn't like the tone of the neighbourhood being lowered."

"By Rose's men friends?"

"Yep."

"Many?"

"A fair variety," Roger said. "Looks as if there were enough to make it pretty obvious what she did. She didn't go out to work regularly, but did a lot of tapestry work and sold it through one or two West End shops, too. Earned a bit, and had a fair income from Government stocks and a few industrials."

"Just wanted to earn pin money in the evenings," the other C.I. remarked. Then his telephone bell rang, and he lifted the receiver quickly. "Carter speaking …"

Roger sifted through the reports.

There were sixty-two houses in Page Street, and nearly half of them were divided into two flats. So the police had made more than a hundred calls that morning, with comparatively little to show for it.

Most of the neighbours had been out, or else in their own back gardens. Elwell was a neighbourhood where the front room was still the parlour, kept for week-ends and special occasions.

West picked up the report from *Fingerprints*. Rose Jensen's prints had been everywhere in the flat, and there were three others which could be photographed, but none of these was in *Records*. The curious thing about the situation was that no papers at the flat gave any indication about the woman's past; there were no letters, and not a single name and address except her bank. The bank manager knew her as a model customer, that was all.

West finished his study, made one or two notes, and then turned to other cases on his desk. It was half an hour before the telephone bell rang.

"West speaking."

"Good morning, sir. Colonel Jay would like to see you."

"I'll come along at once."

"Thank you, sir."

West put down the receiver, but didn't get up immediately. Carter, the only other C.I. present out of the five who shared this large office, glanced across at him as if sensing trouble. The sunlight, striking through an open window, caught West's fair hair, a colour which concealed the increasing grey in it and made him look much younger than his forty-two years. He wasn't called 'Handsome' for nothing.

"Jay?" Carter asked.

"Yes."

"Well, you can't expect 'em all to eat out of your hand, can you?"

"No, I can't can I?" Roger said, and stood up quickly. His grin concealed the surge of irritation he felt at Carter's remark. It wasn't the first of its kind, and it wasn't meant to be taken seriously, yet it stung. Until a few months ago, Roger had probably had the best prospects of any man at the Yard, with the whole-hearted support and liking of the then Assistant Commissioner for Crime, Sir Guy Chatworth. Over the years, he had grown used to being dubbed Chatworth's white-haired boy. Why not? He hadn't given it much thought then, but Chatworth had retired through illness, and soon afterwards a tartness had crept into the voices of some of the other C.I.D. men.

Was it true to say that Carter was 'tart'?

If he was, could he be blamed?

He was nearing fifty, and had only just been promoted to his present rank. Roger, at forty, had been a C.I. for several years. He hadn't noticed it at the time, or hadn't given it much thought, but since Chatworth had gone, he had realised how many older men in the Criminal Investigation Department's service had been passed over for him and other younger men.

Now Colonel Jay was in Chatworth's place.

No one yet knew how to take Jay. There had been some annoyance and perhaps resentment among the senior men who had hoped to step into Chatworth's shoes, for Jay had been brought in from outside, with no intimate knowledge of the Yard. There had been talk of a new broom; hints and suggestions that Chatworth's regime had been too soft, that Chatworth had been too friendly with the senior staff, implications that he had been much too friendly with one or two. If one tried to look at this from the point of view of the Commissioner, it made sense. Results had been good, but if in fact Chatworth had had favourites, it was easy to see that the Commissioner might feel that he ought to bring someone in from outside, and make sure that everyone started from scratch.

None of this greatly worried Roger, but he didn't like the implication that he was a senior C.I. because of Chatworth's influence and friendship, and not because of his qualities and qualifications. It had never been voiced, but Carter's "Well, you can't expect 'em all to eat out of your hand, can you?" had stabbed. A lot of remarks like it stabbed.

Roger didn't look round, but was aware that Carter was looking up at him from under his brows as he went out. No one was in the corridor, and his footsteps echoed. He wished he could shake off the feeling of annoyance and irritation, but it was stronger than ever when he reached the A.C.'s office on the floor above. He found himself smiling wryly, for he felt now as many had felt when tapping at Chatworth's door. Chatworth had scared the lights out of a lot of men, even seniors who should have known better. Perhaps it was only a question of getting to know Jay, too.

Jay had a different secretary from Chatworth, whose secretary had been Big Sister to many Yard men. This one was younger, in the early thirties. She wasn't bad-looking, her manner was a little too sweet, and it was difficult to be sure that she wasn't two-faced.

"Good morning, Mr. West."

"Morning, Miss Foster."

"I'll tell the Colonel you're here."

"Thanks," said Roger. He watched her as she picked up the telephone, listened as she passed on the information primly. Then she said: "Very good, sir," and put down the receiver.

"The Colonel won't keep you many minutes, Mr. West."

"Thanks," Roger said again, and moved towards the window. It overlooked the Embankment, and on a summer's morning, that was quite something to see. There wasn't a ripple on the surface of the Thames, except the wake of two pleasure-steamers on the way upstream, their gaily coloured awnings vivid, their decks crammed with people. Westminster Bridge looked as if it would stay there another two hundred years. Traffic on the bridge and the Embankment was very thick. Little groups of tourists were standing opposite, and taking pictures of Scotland Yard.

Roger expected the telephone or other bell to ring, as a summons. It didn't. After several minutes, he turned to look at Miss Foster, and was startled to see Colonel Jay standing in the doorway between the two offices. Jay's opening of the door must have caught his attention, although he hadn't consciously heard it. He could not fail to see that Jay was studying him. Critically?

There was a moment's awkward pause, and then Roger said: "Good morning, sir."

"Good morning, West. Come in, will you?"

"Yes, sir."

There couldn't be much good in this kind of formality.

The A.C.'s office had changed, too. Chatworth had favoured chromium and glass, Jay was more conventional, and the Office of Works had been quite willing to switch the furniture round. Chatworth's was now in the Yard's secretarial offices. The dark oak here made the room seem smaller than it had been, even dimmed the brightness of the morning. There was Jay's green swivel armchair behind the desk, another armchair in front of it, and two or three high-backs.

"Pull up a chair, and sit down," Jay said.

"Thank you."

"West," began Colonel Jay, without preamble, "will you give me your considered opinion as to the degree of success that we at the Yard achieve against major criminals?"

He had a rather precise, military voice, almost remote; there was obviously a danger that he was a humourless man. To look at, he was not exceptional; his regular features were perhaps a little small, his greying hair was cut very short at the back and sides, and rather crimped on top. He had a weathered complexion and very clear grey eyes; any one suit of Chatworth's would have made two for Colonel Jay, whose waistline was actually concave. He wore tweeds which were cut to fit very tightly, almost moulding the outline of his figure.

Obviously, this was to be a kind of test.

"I think I'd like the question qualified, sir," Roger said.

"Oh? How?"

"By 'major criminals' do you mean professionals who go in for the big stuff, or normally law-abiding individuals who've committed major crimes?"

Was that being 'smart'? It was impossible to judge Jay's reaction, there was nothing at all to go by.

"What is your considered opinion on each?"

"I think we get nearly a hundred per cent of the professionals," Roger answered quietly. "I don't know of many who haven't been inside and aren't likely to go again. There are one or two who've kept out of our hands, usually because we can't get evidence, but they'll slip up one day. If we're thinking of professional crooks after they've committed the crime, I don't think we can ask for much more, sir. We're a long way behind in methods of prevention, though, and we'd need twice as many men in the uniformed branch to get on top of that." Roger spoke with great deliberation; at least Jay would understand that he'd given this thought. "It's difficult to assess success against the ordinary citizen who commits an isolated crime and hopes to get away with it. I would say that some of the crimes committed are never discovered. Of those that are discovered, we get a fair proportion of convictions."

"Are you satisfied with that proportion?"

"Not by any means, sir."

"What proportion of major thefts are unsolved, for instance?"

"About fifty per cent," Roger replied.

"That's very high."

"It's much too high."

"How do you account for it?"

"Delay in discovering the crime is probably the largest single factor, sir."

"What are the other important factors?"

There was a catch here, but Roger didn't see what it was. These were all partly trick questions. He couldn't recall anyone else reporting a catechism like this from Jay, so he had been selected for special treatment.

"Two main ones, I'd say, sir. The first is the ingenuity of the criminal, the other is the difficulty of getting witnesses. Once they know that their evidence is wanted in a big case, they hesitate and often want to back out. It isn't much use subpoenaing an unwilling witness. They don't like the responsibility, and are difficult in court."

"And is that all?"

"There's another factor which is pretty general in all jobs."

"What have you in mind?"

Roger said very cautiously: "The human factor, sir. We make mistakes. I can recall at least two occasions in the past where I have made serious ones, one simply because I didn't see the right angle until too late, the other because at the time I'd been working for forty-eight hours straight, and was too tired."

"Ah," said Jay, perhaps a little more softly. "Wouldn't it have been wise to have handed over to someone else until you had some rest?"

"Very wise."

"Why didn't you?"

"No one else was qualified to handle that particular investigation."

"Were you sure about that, or was it a question of preferring to handle the case yourself, West?"

At least he had come out into the open now; was deliberately needling Roger, implying that he'd kept going on a case longer than he should because he wanted the satisfaction and perhaps the glory of catching his man, Roger's immediate problem became acute. Should he let Jay see that he realised what this was all about, or should he play dumb? The one thing he mustn't do was show annoyance. Nor must he point out that Chatworth had found nothing to complain about in these particular cases.

"It's very difficult to be sure when you are too tired to work properly," Roger said carefully. "We get used to working for long stretches and at high pressure, and usually keep going for as long as we can. If you mean, did I prefer to handle it rather than bring in someone else – no, sir."

"What case was this?"

"The Fortescue murder, three years ago."

"The Fortescue murder, yes." Jay paused. "Give me another considered opinion, West."

"On what subject, sir?"

"Do you think there is any weakness in our organisation, apart from shortage of manpower in certain branches? Weaknesses in training, for instance, or of concentrating too much in the hands of any one person or group of individuals."

"On the contrary, sir."

"I don't quite understand you."

"If anything, I would say that there isn't sufficient concentration."

"Give me an example."

"On my desk at the moment there are reports on seven different cases, all pending. It would be very much more satisfactory if I could concentrate on one or two. I know it isn't always possible, and that's an organisational weakness. Whether other weaknesses would develop if we were able to concentrate more, I don't know."

"I see," said Jay, and there was an edge of sarcasm in his tone. "Is there any one particular case on which you would like to concentrate at the moment?"

"The new cases always seem more attractive than the old ones, sir."

"You mean, the Rose Jensen murder."

"Yes."

"Have you formed any conclusions?"

"None at all," Roger said bluntly. "I haven't even seen the body or the scene of the crime, only studied the reports which were on my desk with a note from Superintendent Cortland."

"On my instructions," Jay said, and moved his chair back and stood up. "I want you to concentrate on the Jensen case. You may pass on all other matters, through Superintendent Cortland, and work exclusively on this. I should like a day-to-day report on your progress."

"Written, sir?"

"No. Verbal."

"Very well, sir," Roger said, already standing up. "Is there anything else?"

"Not now," said Colonel Jay, and nodded dismissal. He didn't speak again until Roger was at the door, when he said: "You'll look for that cyclist first, won't you?"

"I'll look for the cyclist," Roger said expressionlessly. "Good morning, sir." He went out and closed the door, stalked towards the landing and the stairs, his face set very hard, and as he reached the head of the stairs he said explosively: "I'll have that cyclist before the day's out if I have to question a thousand cyclists myself!"

Later, he realised the worst thing was that he couldn't laugh at himself, after saying that. At the time, he meant it. Finding the cyclist of Page Street had become all-important; the elderly man was almost secondary in his mind.

He himself was on trial.

Chapter Four

High Pressure

Carter wasn't in the office when Roger got back. Bill Sloan, also newly promoted, one of Roger's cronies and also a 'favourite' of Chatworth, was there, together with an old-timer, Eddie Day. Eddie, a Cockney, was the Yard's expert on forgery, but had never reached superintendent's rank, a fact which he sometimes blamed on to favouritism. He had a pointed nose, a receding chin and prominent, yellowish teeth, which seemed more protuberant than they really were because he often breathed through his mouth. Now he was studying a cheque through a magnifying glass; it was one of his boasts that he could get results through a glass which others wouldn't get when using *infra red*.

Both men looked up, and stopped what they were doing when they saw Roger.

Sloan didn't speak.

"Wot's 'appened, 'Andsome?" demanded Eddie. "Lost a fortune?"

"Probably lost my stripes," Roger said, deciding that it was better to come out with it, for Eddie would soon suspect the truth. "I've learned that the A.C. has definite ideas of his own."

"Time we had an A.C. like that," Eddie said. He had made similar cracks, but seldom succeeded in annoying Roger; this one annoyed him.

Roger said: "Well, we've got one. Better brush up your *Gross on Criminal Investigation*, Eddie, you might find yourself under cross-examination."

"Strewth, one of those, is he?" Eddie said. "Works by the book. Thanks for the tip, 'Andsome." He turned back to his desk, obviously full of resolve. Roger and Sloan grinned, and somehow Sloan's red, fresh face and clear blue eyes restored Roger's good humour.

"I'm going to see Cortland, and then get out on the Rose Jensen job," Roger said. "I'm to forget the others. You'll probably find them pushed on to your desk, Bill; better have a look through them." He tapped the other pending reports. "If you've any questions, I can answer 'em a bit later."

He gathered up the Page Street papers, and went out.

The talk with Cortland was brief. Roger had two sergeants detailed to help him, and could call on whatever help he thought was necessary.

First he went to see the dead woman on the morgue slab. The morticians had made her look quite peaceful. He checked the medical report, and found that death had undoubtedly been caused by strangulation.

"Any indication that she'd had intercourse in the hour or so preceding death?" Roger asked.

"No."

"That's something. Anything else?"

"Nothing at all – no finger-nail scrapings, if that's what you mean, nothing to suggest that she put up a fight."

"Right, thanks."

"Pleasure."

Roger drove to Page Street in his green Wolseley. The roads were fairly empty, and the journey took him less than fifteen minutes. Brown, one of the two sergeants detailed to work with him, was talking to a uniformed policeman and a little elderly woman, near Number 31. Roger didn't interrupt, but went to the front door, where a constable stood on duty. A few people stood about idly, but there were no newspapermen, nothing to suggest that the case had caught the public fancy.

Ibbetson, the other detective sergeant, was in the dead woman's bedroom. This overlooked a narrow back garden, the gardens of nearby houses and of other houses across the road, which were identical with those in Page Street. A woman was beating a carpet hanging over a clothes-line, and in the garden next door a line was filled with baby's white napkins.

"Good morning, sir."

"Hallo, Ibbetson," Roger greeted. "Having any luck?"

"Nothing new at all, sir," Ibbetson said, with his faintly north-country accent. He had a north-country look, too, a broad, amiable face and rather heavy jowl and eyelids; an elderly face in a young man. "I haven't found a scrap of paper with writing on it, any name and address, anything at all. The woman downstairs says that Rose Jensen kept herself to herself pretty much; often they wouldn't exchange a word for weeks on end. Mutual dislike, I fancy."

"I'll have a word with the downstairs woman – what's her name?"

"A Mrs. Kimmeridge. She lives there with her husband, a London Transport bus driver. Pretty reliable, I'd say."

"Did she have much to say about the various men who came to see Rose Jensen?"

"From what I can judge, she heard more than she saw of them," said Ibbetson. "That's what annoyed her as much as anything else. Probably a lot of hot air."

"Other neighbours?"

"Only found two who noticed anything much, and they agree that there were more men callers than you'd expect."

"Descriptions?"

"The usual, sir—every sort of man from a chap who looked like a lion-tamer to a little fellow with mousy hair. I've come to expect people to be vague, but in this case they seem to take the biscuit!"

"Any description which seems to cover men who've been here several times?" asked Roger.

"Well, yes," said Ibbetson, and tapped the notebook which bulged slightly in the pocket of his unpressed suit. "Only two really stand up – elderly chap, rather fat, who seems to have been once or twice before; and a nice-looking young chap – answers the description of the cyclist, too," Ibbetson declared. "Mrs. K said she saw the cyclist come in but not leave. I should say those two descriptions are pretty sound."

"Let me have a look at what you've written about 'em," said Roger, and held out his hand for the notebook. "Thanks. Good – we'll check with one or two of the neighbours, then go all out for this pair. Who else saw the two men?"

"As a matter of fact, sir, three people noticed the cyclist, but only Mrs. Kimmeridge seems sure he went in. The elderly chap's doubtful, but two neighbours say they definitely saw him, and one says he went in. Had to get a bit sharp with some of them before they'd go that far."

Roger nodded.

"I've spoken to the Divisional copper who saw the cyclist outside Number 31," Ibbetson went on. "He didn't think anything of it at the time."

"Did he see this fat chap?"

"No. Very clear description of the cyclist, though. I've taken this report down *verbatim*."

"Fine," said Roger. "Thanks." He read of a tall, athletic-looking man probably in the late twenties, wearing a brown sports jacket of smooth texture, grey flannel trousers, a pale blue sports shirt, a scarf knotted at the throat, no hat, brown hair cut fairly short, highly-polished brown shoes. The bicycle was an Olympic, light green semi-racer type, probably fairly new. It had red tyres.

"Chap keeps his eyes open," Roger remarked. "How much further have you gone?"

"That's about the lot, sir. There's a great deal of embroidery and tapestry work here; she was good with her needle. Neat and tidy, too – packs everything up well." Ibbetson pointed to some fat cardboard tubes. "All tapestries. I'll find out more about that angle."

"Good," Roger said. "Now go along to Elwell Police Station, and ask them to put the description of the cyclist out on the teletype. A cyclist wouldn't have a very wide radius, so suppose we ask all Divisions within twenty miles to try and trace this chap, putting a special concentration on the Hadworth area. Will you fix that?"

"Yes, sir." Ibbetson was eager.

"What's the woman like downstairs?" Roger asked. "From our point of view, I mean."

"Probably ask you to have a cup of tea," said Ibbetson and grinned.

"All right. Send a constable up here, will you? We won't seal the flat yet."

"Right," said Ibbetson.

Five minutes later, Roger tapped at the front door of the flat below. The two flats in the house shared the same street door, but the one downstairs had a separate front door, close to the foot of the stairs; that was common in many houses of this type. Roger was surprised to find the woman tall, brisk and middle-aged, quite a looker in her way. Her white blouse was nicely filled, her black skirt was rather tight so that it emphasised her flat waist; a good figure for the middle forties. Obviously she had expected visitors and had made up for the occasion.

"Haven't I seen you before somewhere?" she asked, staring intently at Roger; she did not seem unduly impressed by his looks. "Perhaps it's a picture in the papers, but somewhere. Are you coming in?"

"May I, for five minutes?"

"I was just going to make a cup of tea," said Mrs. Kimmeridge; "I usually do about eleven o'clock in the morning." She led the way to a back room which was pleasantly furnished, probably rather more expensively than most of the houses in Page Street. Everything suggested a house-proud woman to whom cleanliness was probably nearer godliness than godliness itself. "I expect you want to ask all the same questions as the other fellows, really."

"I'll try to think up some new ones," Roger said.

Whether they were new or old, she answered freely, confirming everything that Ibbetson had told him, and was quite sure about the young man on the bicycle. He had been there several times.

She seemed less sure about the fat, elderly man – she had seen him in the street and thought she recognised him as a visitor Rose Jensen had had before, but wasn't positive he had come in. In any case, that had been much earlier than the time she had seen the cyclist; she was sure of that. She refrained from criticising Rose Jensen, possibly on the grounds of not speaking ill of the dead.

"Could you identify this cyclist?" Roger asked.

"Oh, yes; no doubt about that. I had a good look at him again last night. I never did like it, but there's a key hanging down inside the street door, and anyone who knows about it can come in. I keep *my* door locked, I can tell you."

"Did you see the cyclist come in?"

"Yes."

"Did you see him go out?"

"No. There was a play on the television, my husband and I always like looking at plays, so we didn't take any more notice. After all, Miss Jensen's business *was* her business, wasn't it?"

"A very charitable point of view," murmured Roger. "Could you be sure of the identity of any of the other people who visited Miss Jensen at any time?"

"Well, honesty is the best policy, my husband and I always say," said Mrs. Kimmeridge, "and I couldn't swear to the others. I might be able to tell you if I'd seen them before, but I don't spend my time spying on a neighbour's callers." She drew herself up, most righteously.

"I'm sure you don't," Roger said.

He left after twenty minutes, and Mrs. Kimmeridge made a point of seeing him to the front door. He had all the known facts clear in his mind when he drove to the local Divisional Headquarters, where a Superintendent named Grey was in charge. Grey had already seen Ibbetson, the teletype call had gone out for the cyclist and the elderly man, everything was in hand.

"Another thing I did, Handsome; thought it might speed things up a bit—I had a word with the Olympic Cycle people. Wondered how many of their models have red tyres. Only one in ten, it turns out; that should help a bit; and what's more they didn't start fitting them as a regular thing until eighteen months ago, so that limits the range."

"First class. Thanks."

"Always glad to prove that the Yard isn't the only place where they grow coppers," said Grey, grinning. He was biggish and elderly, with a good reputation. "Shouldn't think it'll be long before you pick up this cyclist. What do you think happened?"

"You guess."

"Being careful, aren't you? Must be the effect of that new broom I've heard about! Well, it looks pretty clear to me."

"Tell me."

"This Jensen woman has had several beaux on the end of pieces of string," said Grey. "The old man was probably still welcome to her couch because he's in the money. The cyclist obviously hasn't much cash – who'd cycle, if he could afford a car? – and he was young. Last night he saw the old boy had gone, and went in and put his lady love where she couldn't get up to that game again. Wouldn't be the first time it happened."

"Nor the last," agreed Roger solemnly.

"Now what's on your mind?" demanded Grey. "Trying to see more in it than there is, I shouldn't wonder. Let me tell you something I've learned after forty years in the Force, Handsome."

"Most cases have simple answers," Roger said, still solemnly.

"You devil!" grinned Grey. "You've heard me say that before! Well, so they have; don't go tying yourself up into knots because you want to hand the new Jay this case on a platter, just to show him how smart you are."

Roger's smile didn't change, but his mood did.

He left Grey five minutes later, with that last remark still rankling. Grey of all people had no axe to grind. If he or any of the Divisional men had a notion that he, West, would go all out to impress the new A.G., whose fault was it? He himself must have created the impression.

Big head?

Well, this job looked simple, Roger reflected grimly, but no one was going to make him jump to conclusions, after twenty years' experience of the C.I.D.

He drove back to the Yard, arranged for two men to stay at the dead woman's flat, checked other reports, and found three more were in about the cyclist in Page Street last night. There were other reports, one of a taxi, one of two private cars, but none of these had gone to Page Street so far as it was possible to say. Everything pointed to that good-looking cyclist.

Roger put out a call for a taxi-driver who had taken an elderly man to Page Street.

Ibbetson came in, just before one o'clock. Roger was alone in the big office then; two telephones started to ring at the same time. He let them ring.

"How're you doing, Ibby?"

"I've just had a message from Hadworth Hill tube station," Ibbetson said. He was young and eager enough to show excitement. "A taxi-driver there says he saw a cyclist answer this description last night. Recognised him too."

Roger said sharply: "Can he name him?"

"No, but he says he catches a train at half-past eight each week-day, and usually gets home about six o'clock," said Ibbetson. "Two or three of the station staff also recognise the description, and they think the chap had a season ticket to Green Park. That's if he's the same one."

"We want a man at that station from now until we pick him up," said Roger. "I'll lay it on, you keep checking." In his own excitement, he had almost forgotten how essential it was to get quick and conclusive results in this case; had almost forgotten Colonel Jay.

They'd have that cyclist before the day was out.

Half an hour later they had a call from a taxi-driver who had taken a 'fat, elderly man' from Hadworth Station to the Rose and Crown in Elwell High Street, which was two streets away from Page Street. The Rose and Crown would be worth a visit soon.

Chapter Five

Mistake

Michael Quist left his office just after five o'clock and walked briskly towards Green Park station, buying each of the London evening newspapers on the way. Usually he bought only the *Evening Globe*. Usually, too, he hurried to the station and jostled for a place on a train to Piccadilly, changed to the Hadworth line, and was at Hadworth about six. He didn't hurry tonight, but crossed the road and stepped inside Green Park, and scanned the newspapers. He did not see the little man who watched him.

Each front page carried the story.

Each one now said that the police were anxious to interview an elderly man dressed in clerical grey, and a young man aged about twenty-eight, who had been on a cycle near the house in Page Street about nine o'clock last night. The police, each said, believed that they could help them with their inquiries. Even to Quist, who knew very little about police work and procedure, that had an ominous ring; the man who could 'help' was often later arrested.

He did not give much thought to personal danger. He had put in a confidential written report for Gorringe, only yesterday; and once he was questioned by the police he would refer them to his report and the story of his investigation. It was almost certain that Gorringe would contact the police directly he read the report, but he was more likely to send for him, Michael Quist. In any case,

Gorringe had been away for a few days, with influenza, and probably had not returned yet. There was time.

Every hour he could put off taking action, the better. In spite of falling in love with Sybil, he had been driven by conscience to find out all he could, and now felt sure that the defalcations were made at the bank. Charles Henry's behaviour suggested that he was guilty, but there seemed to be others pushing him; otherwise, why was he so afraid?

Before long, the police would find out all about this; would it help anyone, Sybil or her father, if they were told now? It certainly wouldn't help the dead woman.

Quist looked in the general direction of Westminster and Scotland Yard. He knew the Yard buildings as every Londoner did; they held no especial terrors for him. He could walk there in twenty minutes, and tell his story in another ten.

What *was* the best way to help Sybil?

When the blow fell, she would need all the help she could get, and if he was the man who had betrayed her father, how could she turn to him?

That was his only concern: how to ease the coming blow for Sybil.

A shadow of apprehension fell upon him. Supposing Henry killed himself before being arrested; he'd had the look of a man driven to desperation. And what would the police say when they knew that he, Michael Quist, could have stopped that by telling them what he knew?

That was letting his imagination run riot. The police weren't to know how soon he had discovered that the murdered woman and Henry's companion were one and the same. No harm would come from waiting. He might be able to decide what to do.

Could he spend much time with Sybil without telling what he knew?

He went to a telephone kiosk near the Ritz Hotel, and still did not notice the little man who followed him. Sybil's number was in the London dialling area, and he heard the ringing sound going on and on. His heart began to thump, and it wasn't simply because he was going to talk to Sybil. There was at least a chance that her father had been questioned and arrested. Sybil's tone would betray any such disaster, and he would drop everything and rush over to her.

She herself answered. "Hadworth 3412."

Try as he might, Quist couldn't put a natural eagerness into his voice; couldn't stop his heart from thumping.

"Sybil darling?"

"Micky!"

"Hallo, my sweet," he said. "I tried before, but you were out."

"Oh, what a shame! Mother and I were shopping." There was no hint of crisis here.

"And I've been rushed off my feet since; Saxby's are such slave-drivers."

"Aren't they all?"

"I suppose so. How—how are you?"

"Oh, I'm fine."

She sounded gay; in fact she sounded delighted to hear him. Nothing suggested that she even suspected trouble, or that his manner puzzled her. She was just Sybil. He felt quite sure now that he was doing the right thing: must be ready at her side, when the blow fell. After the shock was over, perhaps in a few days, he would tell her that he had been watching her father. Gorringe hadn't yet seen that report, and it might be possible to get it back so that no one need know it had ever been written. At heart, Quist didn't think it would be so easy, but he felt less burdened, and sure that he could help Sybil when the time came.

"Free tonight?" he asked.

"Of course, darling!"

"Let's meet at Richmond," Quist suggested. "We'll have dinner and go on the river for an hour or two; it's just the night for it. A friend of mine has a small boat I can borrow. How does it sound?"

"Wonderful!" Such happiness: and by tonight she might be almost in despair.

"How long will it take you to get there?" Quist asked.

"About half an hour," Sybil replied; "I can use the car."

"Wonderful! Make it half-past six, and if I'm a few minutes late—"

"Don't worry about that, I'll be waiting."

Would she be?

He went towards Piccadilly, for a train to Waterloo and Richmond, hurrying now; and was followed. He bought a ticket at a machine, and went with the jostling crowds towards the trains. The platform was crowded, with many people pushing: and several times he was edged towards the rails. He didn't mind; at all costs he wanted to catch that train.

He heard it rumbling through the tunnel, and as it drew nearer, its lights actually in sight, a man fell against him heavily.

His heart turned over.

The train roared.

He staggered wildly, and a woman screamed; then a youth grabbed at him and pulled him back, as the train flashed by.

"My God," thought Quist, "I must wake up."

He was sweating from the narrowness of the escape, but put it down to his own haste in the crowd. He didn't give a thought to attempted murder.

Sybil was waiting, and showed no sign at all of distress.

She stood by the side of her parents' small Austin, wearing a lemon-coloured, sleeveless dress with a square neckline. She looked beautiful. And she was so much in love that she did not even try to conceal it from him.

It was an hour before Quist even asked after her mother and father.

"Oh, Father got home about eleven last night," Sybil told him. "He'd had a drink or two, and was quite cheerful. Mother was anxious not to upset him, so everything went off quite well. Honestly, Mick, I don't know whether to hate him for what he's done to mother or not. I just hate thinking about it, but—well, I can't say anything to her, can I?"

"Of course not."

"Darling, you needn't worry about it any more," Sybil said. "Please don't."

Not worry!

He knew that he ought to tell her now, then go to the police, but her reaction might be swift and fierce – and she might be left on her own to cope.

Quist said nothing.

It was nearly eleven o'clock when they reached Hadworth, and Sybil slowed down at a turning which led to Quist's street. They had been quiet for the past ten minutes, and now Sybil spoke as if with an effort.

"Which turning do I take?"

"You don't," said Quist. "Drop me near the station; it's only five minutes' walk."

"But—"

"It's better that way," Quist said, quite firmly. If they drove to his flat, if they lost their heads – and that would be so very, very easy – they could spoil the whole future. "Are you free tomorrow?"

"I'm always free," Sybil said, with a catch in her breath. "Mick, it's so—so perfect."

She stopped.

He held her fiercely, kissed her passionately, and felt her straining towards him. It was a kind of all-consuming madness. He had known nothing like it before, and felt sure that she had not.

This was a wide, tree-lined road and it was dark and there were few street lamps; it was a quarter of an hour before Quist said almost roughly: "You must get home, Sybil."

"I know."

"I love you."

"I love you."

Soon he was standing and watching her drive off. He could think of nothing but Sybil as she disappeared; of Sybil as he walked through the poorly lit streets towards his own flat. What would it be like when she got home? Would the police be there? Oh, he was crazy not to have warned her somehow.

He reached the flat where he lived, one of six in a corner house in a narrow street, and lights were on at several of the others. He heard music, but tonight he did not put on his record player, could not bring himself out of the trance, except to remember what horror waited for Sybil when the truth was known. He knew one thing: it would be much, much more difficult to tell the police anything now. He must get the report back from Gorringe's desk, and forget that he had ever seen Charles Henry with that now dead woman ...

It was a little after seven when he woke next morning, so he did not have to hurry to get breakfast and catch his train. The *Gazette*, his morning newspaper, carried a story on an inside page; the police were still looking for the cyclist, but there was no mention of anyone else. Michael felt uneasy, the night's excitement all gone. He left it late, after all, bolted down a boiled egg and some cereal, and had to step out pretty quickly for the station.

He wasn't quite himself. There were things that had been said and had happened last night which had all the quality of a dream. He tried to shake the mood off as he neared the station, with the usual crowd. He saw familiar faces – passengers as well as ticket collectors, newspaper-boys, taxi-drivers, all the daily familiarity of life. He also saw a small man whom he had seen the night before, but couldn't place him, although memory of the near accident made him shudder.

The little man went ahead, towards the platform, and Quist noticed two heavily-built men standing by the ticket-collector's booth as he flashed his season ticket, and it wasn't until he was past, and putting the ticket away, that he realised that the two men had stepped up on either side of him.

"Excuse me, shy can you spare a minute?" The speaker had a north-country accent.

"Sorry," said Quist; "I'm late this morning, I must catch my train. If we can talk as we go I'd be glad to. What's it all about?"

"I'll have to ask you to step on one side," said the north-countryman, taking something out of his pocket. "I am a detective officer from Scotland Yard, and would like you to answer a few questions."

Quist stopped short. Someone behind nearly bumped into him, and glowered. The policemen were on either side, hemming him in.

The card, in front of his eyes, said clearly: Criminal Investigation Department, Metropolitan Police, and there was a printed name on it. Detective Sergeant someone.

One of the men held his arm.

"There's a quiet spot along here, sir," said the north-countryman, almost too respectfully, and led the way.

So far, Quist hadn't said a word. He needed no telling what this was all about, but still couldn't decide what to say.

"This is all very well," he managed to protest at last, "but I shall be late at my office, and—"

"We'll telephone your apologies," said the north-countryman, as they reached a spot near the up platform where very few people were about. "Would you mind telling me where you were on Monday evening? The evening before last?"

At ten o'clock that Wednesday morning, Roger West heard the telephone on his desk, and damned it for ringing. He had just been told that the cyclist was downstairs, with Ibbetson and a detective officer, and was on the point of going to see him. He picked up the receiver and said snappily: "West here."

"Good morning, Mr. West," said Miss Foster brightly. "The Colonel would like you to come and see him at half-past ten."

"Right; thanks," said Roger, and rang off; then wondered if he had been too curt. He grinned at himself, but wasn't too sure that he could laugh Miss Foster off. He gathered up several papers, and hurried from his desk. Half an hour might be ample, or it might be far too short a time for an interview with the cyclist named Michael Quist.

The door opened as he reached it.

"'Alio, 'Andsome," greeted Eddie Day. "'Ow's tricks?" Something had obviously pleased Eddie, he was seldom as expansive as this. "Remember that ten-bob job? Good as the real things, they were; been a pain in the neck for over six months. Just caught the beggar. Know 'ow I did it? You'd never believe."

Minutes were flying, and there were too few already. But the delight in Eddie's face was so vivid that it would be cruel not to give him a little longer to exult.

"How did you, Eddie?"

"The paper," Eddie exploded. "Must be a flaw in the paper-making plant, there was always a tiny black mark in the top right 'and corner, near the number. Always made a point of looking for this, I did. Then I was 'aving a dekko at some share stertificates." Eddie could never pronounce 'certificate' properly. "Anything on the same kind of paper was all right for me, and gor-blimey, there it was! Same paper, so I made a bee-line for the same printer. Little cove, in Chelsea. Got him 'ung, drawn and quartered. 'Ow about it?"

"Wonderful!"

"Put me in good with His Nibs, this will," Eddie said, rejoicing.

Roger said: "Fine," as heartily as he could, and hurried out. The waiting-room was two floors down; he waited for the lift, thinking it would be quicker, and it was an age coming; when it came it was crowded.

He reached the waiting-room at last. It was ten minutes past ten. The window was so made that it was possible to see the people inside, without them seeing out. On the outside was a kind of ante-room, where Ibbetson waited. At times his slow, deliberate voice and manner could be the most irritating thing at the Yard.

"I haven't much time now," Roger said. "Just want a word with this chap. What do you make of him?"

"If you ask me, he looked as if he would throw himself under a train when we picked him up," said Ibbetson. "He wasn't any more surprised than a father would be about his baby."

"Has he admitted he was in Page Street?"

"Yes, and claims he didn't go into the house," said Ibbetson. "I don't think there's much doubt he's a liar. I thought I'd not ask him too much until you came."

"Good, thanks," said Roger, and moved towards the door. "Was he difficult?"

"Argued a bit at first, that's all."

"Got anything with his dabs on?"

"My cigarette case." Ibbetson looked almost smug.

"Get 'em checked at *Records*, and with those taken at Page Street will you?"

"Yes," The Sergeant went off.

Roger had caught a glimpse of a uniformed constable through the one-way window, and as he went in, his man turned to greet him, whilst the cyclist named Michael Quist stood up from an armchair; he had been perched on the edge. The constable said: "Good morning, sir."

" 'Morning, Evans. Leave us until I call, will you?"

"Very good, sir."

Quist's tension was quite obvious, and meant very little; most men would be tense if they were at the Yard under any kind of suspicion. He was a presentable-looking man, probably nearer thirty than the reports said. He had a good complexion and some tan, and was obviously very fit – the kind of man who looked after himself. His clothes were immaculate, he wore a light grey suit, his collar was laundry-fresh, and he was a careful shaver.

Roger shook hands.

"Sorry to have to bring you here, Mr. Quist; but we hope you can help us."

Quist said: "I've told the other man the simple truth, and he obviously doesn't believe me. I was out for an evening cycle ride." His voice was pleasant but just now rather stilted.

If ever he had wanted plenty of time with a man, Roger did with this one. This wasn't an interrogation to be hurried, and it had been a mistake to see Quist before going to the A.C. He had made a double mistake, for he had come here now because he hoped to have hot news for Jay.

Whenever one allowed oneself to be pushed out of one's normal stride, things went wrong.

"I don't think anyone has jumped to any conclusions," Roger said. "Certainly I haven't. I'm here alone because a confidential talk can't be used at any time – your word would be as good as mine in any court of law. My name's West, Chief Inspector West."

"I've heard of you," Quist declared.

"Never know whether to be pleased or sorry when I hear that," said Roger, almost briskly. Promptly he reminded himself that he mustn't hurry; undoubtedly Quist wanted nursing along. He had to decide pretty quickly what to do, though: he couldn't get half-way, and then stop.

"I want to make one thing clear," Quist said. "I know nothing about that woman or her murder. Nothing at all."

Roger said slowly: "If you don't, you've nothing to fear." And as he spoke he studied Quist, and saw in the man's expression something which suggested that he had some cause for fear; it was easy to understand why Ibbetson had jumped so quickly to a conclusion.

Roger put a finger on a bell-push, without explaining why, and when the constable put his head round the door, said almost casually: "Have a message sent to the Assistant Commissioner and tell him I'm very sorry, but I'll be late, will you?"

The constable looked as if he hadn't heard aright.

"Colonel *Jay*, sir?"

"Yes."

"Er, very good, sir," P.C. Evans said, and withdrew; obviously he thought that Roger had had a mental black-out, and was back in the spacious days of Sir Guy Chatworth.

Well, it was done, and Jay could like or dislike it. The first consideration was the job, and Quist was a big part of the job. Hurriedly or carelessly handled now, the case might fall down. So the Colonel could wait and Roger could put him out of his mind.

It wasn't easy; in fact it was rather like conducting the examination with an unseen presence in the room. Roger couldn't even be sure that he was assessing Quist properly. He was soon quite sure that Quist had a lot on his mind, if not on his conscience.

"Now ... began Roger, as if he had all the time in the world.

"I'm sorry, but I've nothing to say that I haven't said already," Quist declared. "I was out for an evening cycle ride, called at the Rose and Crown for a drink, and then cycled round to see where the roads led to."

"Why did you stop in Page Street?"

"If I did, it was only to light a cigarette."

"Why stop outside that particular house?"

"I don't know where I stopped."

"How well did you know Rose Jensen?"

"I didn't know her. I've never seen her, to the best of my knowledge. And I've nothing more to add," Quist said flatly.

Roger wished he could take one swift look into this man's mind ...

Quist thought: "If I tell him the truth now and he checks with Gorringe, I'll be out of trouble, but Sybil will be in as deep as she can be."

He knew that he was being stubborn, but he'd made his decision. The police were bound to get on to Henry soon, anyhow. For all he knew, they might have had him at the Yard.

The man West asked in his clipped, assured way: "How long did you stop to light this cigarette?"

"I don't even remember doing it."

"Are you a heavy smoker?"

"Er—no."

"Do you usually smoke while cycling?"

"Sometimes."

West didn't press the point, just let it add to Quist's uneasiness, and then asked abruptly: "Did you see anyone else in Page Street?"

"Well—I suppose there were people about."

"You *suppose*?" That was almost a bark.

"I didn't notice anyone in particular," Quist said, and then added almost gruffly: "There was an oldish man; I do remember him."

"Had you ever seen him before?" West asked, and then went on abruptly: "A fattish man, wearing clerical grey?"

So they *were* on to Henry, Quist thought: he could safely keep quiet.

"I slipped up somewhere there," West reflected. "He's cheered up a lot."

He was so intent on Quist that he had completely forgotten Colonel Jay.

"Oh, Cortland," said Colonel Jay to the senior Superintendent, "is it West's habit to break appointments with his seniors, do you know?" The precise voice was quite without expression.

"Never know him do it without cause," said Cortland, shortly.

"But it's not uncommon?"

He was a most difficult man to dissemble with, Cortland knew; every interview with him was rather like being a witness at a court-martial.

"I think we can say that he always puts the job first, sir," he said, and wasn't very happy about the compromise.

The Colonel simply nodded, and turned away.

Chapter Six

Identification Parade

It was impossible to mistake the greater confidence in Quist's eyes, and Roger felt sure that the cause of it turned on the elderly man. Perhaps the wise thing was to let it pass, try to get a line on that man and then tackle Quist again. Roger wanted results quickly, but the facts had to be right: he mustn't fall down on his first job with Colonel Jay.

"Now let's go over one or two things again," he said patiently, and went through the same questions, getting the same answers.

"Are you sure Miss Jensen was a stranger to you?"

"Positive."

"Had you ever been to Page Street before?"

"I didn't even know it was Page Street!"

"It won't help at all if you lie."

"I'm not lying," Quist said curtly.

Roger had a mental picture of Mrs. Kimmeridge, with her white blouse and black skirt, her talkativeness, her steady, ready hand with the teapot. She was the kind of witness it would be a joy to put in the box: quite clear in what she said, most impressive to both judge and jury. She had told him that a man answering Quist's description had visited Rose Jensen several times. Prove Quist a liar once, and he would be suspected in everything he said.

"Very well," Roger said, and still spoke easily. "Let's leave that for a moment. Had you ever been to Page Street before?"

"No."
"Had you ever met Miss Jensen?"
"*No!*"

There was a sharp ring at the telephone which stood on a small table in the corner of the room, after Quist's last 'no'. "Sorry," Roger said, and stepped towards it, acutely conscious of the fact that Quist was watching him intently: "Hallo?"

"Ibbetson here," the detective sergeant said. "Quist's fingerprints weren't at Rose Jensen's flat, sir."

Roger said: "Pity. Anything else?"

"No."

"Thanks," said Roger.

He rang off and turned round.

There was no doubt in his mind that Quist was desperately anxious, and in an odd way Roger himself was glad about the negative report. You could try to be as dispassionate as possible, but couldn't avoid personal prejudice one way or the other; it could get in the way and distort one's perspective.

He liked Quist.

"How long do you think you need to consider this matter, Mr. Quist?"

"I've nothing more to say."

"Then we'll have to ask you to stay for a while," Roger said. "If you change your mind, tell the constable. I'll be in the building most of the morning." He nodded curtly, and as he went out the constable slid into the room, as if to make sure that Quist did no injury to himself. Quist wasn't in that kind of mood, though; he was a complete puzzle.

Roger lit a cigarette and stood in the ante-room, drawing slowly on the cigarette. It was twenty minutes to eleven, and he was beginning to think that he had put Jay off unnecessarily. Damn Jay! If Chatworth had been upstairs, Roger would have called him, and almost certainly been told to get the essential jobs done first.

There was a telephone handy: so he telephoned Miss Foster.

"No, Mr. West, the Colonel is not here. He is at a conference with the Commissioner, and is not expected back until twelve o'clock. I'll tell him that you asked to see him."

"Thanks," said Roger heavily.

His cigarette was half-smoked, and was burning his tongue a little. He walked slowly upstairs. Jay couldn't have allowed him many minutes' grace – or else had left that message to teach him, Roger, that he couldn't be trifled with. What was needed were results; something to justify the delay. Was there any way to get them fast?

Roger was about to enter his office when he saw Ibbetson. "Anything special for me, sir?"

"Yes, Ibby; I'd like to get this one over quick. Go to Page Street, and ask Mrs. Kimmeridge if she'll come here to help us with an identification. Try and get at least one of the other people who saw this cyclist in Page Street the night before last. Then lay on an identification parade – better have that laid on for a quarter to twelve."

"Right!" Obviously Ibbetson wanted action, too.

"Fine," said Roger. "Where's Brown?"

"Checking that Quist does work at Saxby's, and live at 10 Mayhew Road, trying to get a general line on him."

"In the sergeant's room?"

"Yes."

Roger nodded, passed the C.I.'s door and hurried round the corner. Three or four sergeants, all big men, were in a small room which was crowded with desks. Detective Sergeant Brown, the other man working on this job, was a plumpish, brown-clad man with brown hair spread very thin; his pale skull showed through in places. He was making notes, and stopped immediately when he saw Roger.

"How're you doing?" Roger asked.

"Quist is what he says he is, sir," Brown said. "One of the accountants at Saxby's of Piccadilly, training in the secretary's office for a higher position. They have a very high opinion of him. He's worked there since he left school, grammar school, at the age of sixteen – that's eleven years ago. Did his two years' national service, and they kept the job open for him. Got quite a future, they say."

"Who'd you see?"

"Chap named Gorringe."

"Oh, he's there, is he?" Roger said.

"Just got back to work after a dose of 'flu," Brown told him.

"That squares," Roger said. "He have anything else to say about Quist?"

"Seemed to have a pretty high opinion of him."

"Hm," said Roger musingly. "What about Quist's home?"

"His parents died several years ago; he's lived at a small flat in Mayhew Street, Hadworth, for the past six years. A kind of service flat – one of six in a converted house. He has an independent income, too; don't know how much yet. Careful with his money. Doesn't drink much; mostly beer when he does. Plays a bit of cricket for Saxby's, more tennis, golf, rugby. No special girl friend until recently."

Roger said sharply: "Any details about her?"

"No. I had a chap go round to the flat, and a woman who looks after all six apartments lives in the one downstairs. She says Quist's had his girl friends, but there's been no funny business. Then about a month ago he started going steady – out most evenings and weekends, sprucing himself up a bit when he does go out." Brown gave a resigned-looking smile. "All the usual signs."

"We want to know more about that girl friend," urged Roger. "Just who she is and where she lives and where we can get hold of her in a hurry. I want to know if he was with her the night before last."

"Right, sir," Brown said.

Roger went back to his own office, to find Eddie Day holding up a telephone, and saying in a complaining voice: "Well, I don't know where 'e is, so—oh, 'old on a minute, 'e's just come in." He held the telephone out to Roger. "Grey of 'Adworth," he said querulously. "Anyone would think the world would come to an end if 'e couldn't find you."

"Thanks, Eddie," Roger said. "Hallo, what's on your mind out in the suburbs?"

"Got your fat, elderly chap," Grey said promptly, and his voice betrayed satisfaction. "One of the customers at the Rose and Crown knows him. Chap named Charles Henry, chief cashier at the Southern National Bank, Hadworth. Goes in every now and again for a nip; a lot of bank officials like to have their liquor where they aren't likely to bump into their own customers."

"Talked to him yet?" asked Roger.

"No, thought we'd better leave you something to do," Grey said. "But it looks as if he was in the pub when the Jensen woman was killed."

"Check closely, will you?" Roger pleaded. "I've got a parade coming up, and then I'll nip over and see Henry."

The telephone bell rang again almost as Roger put the instrument down. He lifted it quickly, and the operator said: "I've a message from Sergeant Ibbetson, sir. He says that he is about to leave Page Street with Mrs. Kimmeridge and a Mrs. Evans."

"Right, thanks." Roger nodded.

At least they could stage the identification parade before twelve, and he would have evidence of quick, decisive work to show Colonel Jay. He would make time to go and see this bank cashier, too.

A little before a quarter to twelve, eleven men had assembled in the courtyard near the police station at Cannon Row, across the way from New Scotland Yard. They were all young or youngish men, mostly dressed in light grey or in flannels and sports jackets, and most were bare-headed. They had been accosted in the street by soft-voiced detectives and asked to come and help, and were all curious enough to be willing. They stood in a line, a yard or two from the big wall of the police station, a little self-conscious and uncertain of themselves.

Michael Quist saw them when he entered the yard with the detective named West and another man he hadn't seen before. West had asked him if he had any objection to co-operating; he had agreed to do whatever was wanted. He realised what was going to happen as soon as he saw the line of men, and it annoyed and exasperated rather than angered him. He had admitted being in Page Street; there was no reason why he should stand in an identification parade to give added 'proof'. The niceties of the laws of evidence did not occur to him. He didn't protest, just walked towards the line of men.

"If you'll stand in the middle," West said, in his pleasant way. "That's right; thanks." He glanced along the line of men. "Thank you for your co-operation, gentlemen; we won't keep you many minutes."

A woman came from the Yard, accompanied by a plainclothes detective. Quist had not seen her before. It was unnerving to stand here, knowing that everyone else realised that he was the suspect – everyone, that was, except this woman.

She walked along the line, tall, well-built, bosomy.

Most of the men were not given a second glance. One or two suffered a closer scrutiny, but the only man who really caught the attention of the woman was Michael Quist. She didn't speak, but went away with the plainclothes man. An older woman came next, and except that she was more nervous, acted in very much the same way.

When she had gone, West went back to the Yard building, with Quist, and left him in the waiting-room again.

Quist realised that he might be feeling unduly sensitive, but he fancied that West's manner was colder and less friendly.

The little woman from 30 Page Street, nearly opposite Number 31, identified Michael Quist as the cyclist of last evening without hesitation. She said that she couldn't be sure, but didn't remember seeing him go into the house. Roger sent her home in a police car, and then talked to Mrs. Kimmeridge. There was a gleam in this woman's eyes, almost like the light of battle, and she talked even more freely than before.

"... oh, yes, no doubt at all, that was the man. I knew when I was half-way across the yard, I was that certain. He's been in the house half-a-dozen times at least. I even felt sorry for him, because even if she *is* dead, Rose Jensen was a good forty – it wouldn't surprise me to learn that she was forty-five. And he's not much more than a boy! I pray God nothing like this ever happens to a son of *mine*."

Roger evaded the bait; if he inquired about her family she would take a lot of stopping.

"Thank you very much, Mrs. Kimmeridge. And you'd be prepared to swear to this man as a frequent visitor to Miss Jensen, in court if necessary?"

"There's no need to be frightened of the truth," declared Mrs. Kimmeridge downrightly. "The truth will out, that's what I always say, and as true as I'm sitting here, that young man was with Rose Jensen the night before last for the *sixth* time at least. I'll swear it before the Highest Court of all."

It did not occur to Roger that she was lying.

Jay wasn't yet back.

Roger went along to see Quist again, and it was obvious that the identification parade had shaken the other man; he was nothing like so sure of himself, and probably more vulnerable than he had been before.

"Mr. Quist, I think it's time you told me the simple truth," Roger said sharply. "I now know you were in Page Street for several minutes on Monday evening, and I have reason to believe you knew Rose Jensen intimately."

"I didn't know her at all," Quist said doggedly.

"How well do you know Mr. Charles Henry?" Roger asked without warning.

That was the question which gave him what he wanted. He could see Quist's resolve weakening, and did not think it would be long before Quist talked.

Quist thought gloomily: "There's no point in keeping quiet any longer."

He told the whole truth, quietly and convincingly, and could not complain about the attention which West paid to the story.

"Let's get this straight," Roger said, when it was told. "You held back with all this because you didn't want to involve Henry or his daughter?"

"I was only interested in Sybil Henry," Quist replied.

"You were withholding important information from us, and that can get you into plenty of trouble," Roger said, but he didn't labour the point. "What about this report to Saxby's?"

"I put it on Mr. Gorringe's desk on Monday morning. He was away with 'flu."

"Who were the companies concerned and what kind of fraud was involved?"

"Several companies, including Thomas Cole, the coal-and-oil people, Edgers', who supply all Saxby's stationery, Marshall's …" Quist gave the list readily enough, and Roger made notes. "In some cases cheques had been altered—"

"Recently?"

"Within the past few weeks."

"What amounts?"

"Always several hundred pounds."

"What else did you find?"

"Nothing."

"Why did you first suspect Henry?"

"He's the man who usually deals with Saxby's queries, and he seldom misses even a trifle. But he'd passed cheques which even I could see had been altered."

"Good point," Roger nodded.

"I got to know Sybil so as to check on her father," Quist went on. "I wish to God I hadn't, I felt such an utter swine."

"Will you swear that you saw Henry go into Number 31 Page Street?" Roger demanded.

"I don't know that I want to involve—" Quist began. "This isn't a time for sentiment," Roger interrupted. "This man may be a killer, and killers often strike twice. Will you swear to it?"

Quist gave way.

"If necessary."

"Did you go into the house?"

"No."

"Positive?"

"Absolutely positive," Quist said.

But he had lied, earlier; once a liar often a liar?

And in any case there was the clear and damning evidence of Mrs. Kimmeridge.

If this statement of a report to Saxby's was confirmed, it would make Quist's story look much better, but it would not necessarily clear him of the murder charge. He might have killed and be ready to switch suspicion on to Henry, no matter how reluctantly, if driven into a corner.

Roger still liked the man. If it could be proved that Henry had gone into that house—

One reliable witness to corroborate Quist's story would throw the case wide open again.

Roger left Quist, went up to his office and immediately put a call in to Saxby's. He glanced through some reports, and it was five minutes before the operator called him.

"Mr. Gorringe is on the line, sir."

"Thank you," Roger said. "Mr. Gorringe—"

"I was going to get in touch with you at the Yard," Gorringe interrupted at once. He had a deep, strong voice. "Is it true that you're holding Mike Quist on some serious charge?"

"He's being questioned, sir," said Roger.

"What's he supposed to have done?" asked Gorringe, and then gave a deep laugh. "I can hardly expect an answer to that, I suppose. Can I speak to him?"

"I'll gladly give him a message."

"All right," said Gorringe. "Tell him we'll back him all the way, and our legal department is at his disposal."

"I'll tell him," promised Roger. "Have you studied the report which Mr. Quist left on your desk?"

There was a moment's pause, before Gorringe said as if in surprise: "What report? I haven't—hold on a minute, though. I've been off duty for a day or so. Miss Gill! "—he sounded further away—"have you seen any special report from Mr. Quist? ... Eh? ... Oh, all right." He was louder again. "No report's been here, Superintendent. What's all this about?"

"I'll let you know as soon as I can," Roger said quickly.

Had Quist lied?

Or had that report been stolen?

If so, by whom?

Roger sent a sergeant to talk to Gorringe's secretary, and find out who had had access to Gorringe's office and desk. Several members of the company had, it proved, as well as a cashier from the Southern National Bank, at Hadworth, who came on a weekly call to settle queries.

Charles Henry.

"Charles Henry, you're next," Roger said softly.

The shopping district of North Hadworth was pleasant, with wide roads, grass verges, trees which gave plenty of shade. The shops were nearly all in pseudo-Tudor style, and on a corner was the branch of the Southern National Bank where Charles Henry worked. It was unexpectedly large, and a cashier, one of eight behind the counter, said at once: "I'll see if Mr. Henry's free, if you'll wait a minute, sir. The manager is on holiday, and Mr. Henry is deputising for him."

"Thanks," said Roger.

He had to wait only three minutes; then a message came that Henry would see him. He was ushered into a small but well-furnished room, one likely to inspire confidence in most of the bank's customers. So was Charles Henry, who looked the part of manager well enough.

He sat behind a large polished walnut desk. Folded on it was the *Financial Times*; there were two telephones, an ink-stand and a few oddments, but nothing else. Henry sat there, hardly plump enough to be called fat, rather Buddha-like in his immobility, pale hands folded across his paunch, clean-shaven, with thinning, close-cut hair still almost black, and belied the lines at his face which betrayed his age as over sixty. He had a set smile, and Roger thought that his eyes were veiled, as if he was making sure that he didn't give anything away.

"Good morning." He made a gesture of getting up, and held out his hand. "I understand that you would like to see me on business, Mr. West."

"On police business, Mr. Henry. I am Chief Inspector West." Roger came out with his vital question swiftly: "Do you know a Miss Rose Jensen, sir?"

Henry didn't move an inch as he said: "No."

It came out almost too flatly: as if he had been waiting to utter the denial. He pursed his lips a little, and breathed rather heavily through his nose.

"Did you visit a house in Elwell on Monday night, sir?"

"I did not."

"When you left your own home on Monday evening, where did you go, Mr. Henry?" Roger asked, with studied politeness. Just as he had taken to Quist, so did he dislike what he saw of Henry, and what he judged of Henry's attitude.

"To Elwell, for a drink," Henry said. "I—I have every right to go wherever I wish."

"Aren't there any public-houses nearer your home than Elwell?"

"I prefer not to be seen drinking in public too near my bank."

"What public-house did you visit, sir?"

"The Rose and Crown."

"What time did you arrive?"

"I really cannot see what right you have to ask me these questions," Henry said, "and I am answering them only out of a sense of public duty, because I do not want you to waste your time or the public's money. I arrived about half-past eight, and left at about twenty-past ten."

"Were you there all the time?"

"I was."

Henry spoke as if he knew that the statement could be proved, but there was wariness in his eyes, perhaps even a hint of fear. But he had his emotions under control, and it wouldn't be easy to break him down. This wasn't the moment to overdo pressure, and Roger stood up.

"Very well, Mr. Henry. I may have to ask you to repeat your statement formally, later."

"I have no objection to repeating the truth," Henry declared, with heavy dignity.

Roger went out. The cashier who had ushered him into the manager's office was waiting and watching, as if making sure he didn't miss anything there was to see. The other cashiers stared Roger's way, too. Roger nodded curtly, almost reached the door to the sunlit street, then turned round on his heel and hurried back to the office.

He opened the door abruptly.

Henry was sitting in exactly the same position, but his eyes were the eyes of a badly frightened man. He had no colour at all.

If his statements could be fully corroborated, what was on his mind?

Had Quist seen him enter Number 31 Page Street? Or was Quist out to damn this man?

Chapter Seven

Arrest

The Assistant Commissioner sat in his big chair behind his big desk, his face quite without expression as he looked at Roger, who had not been invited to sit down. If Jay kept him standing, it would be the worst possible sign; surely the man couldn't be such a boor.

"Sit down, Chief Inspector," Jay said at last.

"Thank you, sir. I'm sorry that I was delayed this morning. I was interviewing a man in connection with the Jensen murder."

"Very well. With what results?"

"Satisfactory, I think, sir. The man, by the name of Michael Quist ..." Roger didn't waste words, but was not too formal. Jay had already shown interest in the cyclist, and the case against Quist seemed to grow stronger in the telling, particularly because of Mrs. Kimmeridge's evidence. But Roger couldn't get any guide as to Jay's reaction; it was like looking into the face of a statue. "... and in view of the spontaneous evidence of both women, I think that it would be a mistake to let Quist go, for the time being."

Jay said: "I see. Have you charged him?"

"No, sir."

"Do you think the evidence is strong enough for a charge?"

"Yes, sir. On Mrs. Kimmeridge's evidence, he was there after this elderly man arrived, whether that was Henry or not, and didn't leave again until about half-past nine. The elderly man wasn't seen to leave by anyone. The medical evidence is that Rose Jensen died at about nine o'clock the night before last. We can safely allow an hour on either side, and say that death took place between eight and ten o'clock. On the present evidence, and in the absence of anything to prove that anyone else went to the flat after Quist, I would hold him. If the elderly man was in fact Henry, the evidence from the barman and customers at the public-house is bogus, but it's not very probable."

"It's conceivable," Jay said thinly. "Has Quist made a statement?"

"Yes, sir, in great detail." Roger explained, and told Jay of the missing report.

"I fail to see how that affects the murder issue," said Jay. "It might concern the motive, of course, but beyond offering Quist a plausible reason for following Henry, it seems to do nothing else. You are giving full attention to the opportunity Quist certainly had, I hope."

"Yes, sir."

"Beyond this Mrs. Kimmeridge's evidence, is there any evidence that Quist went into the house?"

"No, sir. And there's no sign of his fingerprints inside, but any man who went in with intent to kill might wear gloves, or wipe any prints away, so the defence couldn't make much of that. I'd like to establish Quist's association with the woman, if possible, as that's a key point, but I think it could be done after we've held Quist. Holding him would be quite justified."

"Although he had weighty legal aid at his disposal?"

"If I didn't think there was a good *prima facie* case against Quist I wouldn't recommend holding him, sir. It's not strong enough for the Public Prosecutor's office yet, but no legal obstacle to a charge exists."

"Very well. Charge Quist at whatever you consider the appropriate time. I would like a written summary of your reasons for making a charge, and of Quist's reaction when charged."

"Very good, sir."

"Thank you," Jay said. "And check the bank cashier, Henry."

Was he just a cold fish?

Or was this a case of personal antipathy?

One of the big troubles was that Jay upset Roger's balance and sense of humour. That was restored a little when he reached the lift, and heard Ibbetson, on the landing below, saying exasperatedly: "Where the hell is he? I get the juiciest bit of news for a week, and what does he do? Run out on me. He—"

"You talk too much, Ibby," another man said.

The lift came up, with three sergeants in it. Ibbetson saw Roger, and flushed as red as a rose of Lancaster.

As Roger reached his desk he sat on a corner and asked: "What's so juicy, Ibby?"

"Remember those cardboard tubes and boxes at Rose's place, where she kept her wools and tapestry oddments. All marked 'supplied by Pegg and Company'?" Ibbetson said.

"Yes."

"I checked them, and found she got 'em direct from Pegg's. I shopped around a bit, and a girl at the store where she got her wools says she told her that she got these tubes and cartons from Pegg's free, because Pegg was her cousin. I called the firm, and the chap Pegg admitted it. He says Rose changed her name, so he didn't recognise Jensen, and his paper didn't carry a photo. He's coming to see you this afternoon; I laid it on. Hope that was all right."

"Yes." Everything was falling like manna from heaven. "How did Quist crop up?"

"Oh, Pegg didn't name Quist, just said that there had been a boy friend who was giving trouble, a jealous one or something. He's a bit vague, and says he didn't know Rose very well. I asked him if he knew this boy friend, and he said he'd met him a couple of times, once at Rose's flat and once at the Angel, in Chelsea. In between those occasions, Rose told him she was having trouble. The boy friend's name was Mike – Pegg didn't know the surname – and she meant to break with him as soon as she could. Asked for a description, Pegg described Quist to a T. Which reminds me, sir, we ought to get some photographs of Quist."

"And Henry. We'll get 'em done at once," promised Roger. "How's your shorthand?"

"It'll stand up."

"I want to go down and see Quist now," said Roger. "The A.C. says it's all right to charge him." He turned towards the door with Ibbetson on his heels, and then saw the door open and plump Brown came in, showing more animation than usual; he had even forgotten to tap.

He pulled up short.

"What have you got?" Roger demanded.

"Quist's girl friend," replied Brown with deep satisfaction. "Picked it up at the second go; never known a job run so smoothly! Name of Henry, daughter of a bank cashier; lives at North Hadworth when she's at home. She has a job as a travelling beauty specialist, goes round to exclusive shops and stores demonstrating Creem Beauty Preparations. She met Quist at the Hadworth Tennis Club; he joined a few weeks ago."

So Quist had told some of the truth.

"Where's Sybil Henry now?" Roger asked.

"At her home this week, on holiday. Her father's got a nice house, small car, everything just about as you'd expect, Suburban idyll," Brown went on smugly.

"Could be," Roger agreed. "I want Henry watched, anyhow." He told Brown what he knew, and then went on: "Did you see that barman at the Rose and Crown?"

"Yes, sir. He's quite definite that Henry was there from eight-thirty or so till closing time. I've seen two customers, and although they're not so definite, they saw Henry there most of the evening after they arrived, about eight o'clock."

"And we know she wasn't dead at eight," Roger mused. "I'll go and charge Quist. If he knows anything else to help him, he'll talk all right. Brown, nip along to my desk, and take one copy of the names and addresses of four firms you'll find there along to Superintendent Carling of the Fraud Squad, and ask him for a detailed report on all the firms. We want it down quickly."

"Right, sir!" Brown was glad to be on the move again.

Roger went downstairs, and let the door close on the policeman who had been with Quist. Quist had been here for nearly four hours, and undoubtedly it was getting on his nerves; that wasn't surprising.

He looked more touchy, and as if he could easily lose his temper. He was wary, too, when he saw Ibbetson. The sergeant went to the telephone table, sat down, and took out his notebook.

"Now, Mr. Quist," Roger said, in a tone as dispassionate as ever, "I'll be glad if you'll tell us again everything you can about your reasons for going to Page Street, what you did there, and where you went afterwards. Take your own time."

Quist said, in quick, abrupt tones: "I have decided not to make any further statement until I've been able to talk to a solicitor. I hope there's no objection to that."

"None at all," said Roger smoothly. "You are fully entitled to legal aid. In fact Mr. Gorringe has put the Saxby Company's legal advisers at your disposal. But I want to advise you that it will be in your best interests to state categorically your reasons for going to Page Street, and to state where you went afterwards. There is no question of compulsion; I'm simply expressing my own opinion."

At mention of Gorringe, Quist's eyes had lit up; now he was smiling, although he said: "I'll see my solicitor first, please."

"Very well, Mr. Quist, it will be arranged. Meanwhile, it is my duty to charge you with the murder of a woman named Rose Jensen at her flat at 31 Page Street, Elwell, on the evening of Monday August 9th of this year, and it is my further duty to advise you that anything you say may be written down and used as evidence at your trial."

Ibbetson opened his notebook.

Quist had gone very pale.

"I know nothing about the murder," he said. "You are quite wrong."

"Very well, Mr. Quist; that will be noted. How long had you known Rose Jensen?"

"I tell you that I didn't know her. I saw her last night for a minute or two in a window, that's all."

"Was she by herself?"

"I've said all I intend to say until I have legal advice," Quist said flatly.

"Very well," said Roger. "Do you want us to inform anyone where you are?"

"No."

"Not even Miss Sybil Henry?"

Quist lost what little colour he had left, and clenched both his hands.

"That got under his guard," Ibbetson said with deep satisfaction. "He's damned touchy where this Sybil Henry is concerned." They were walking along the passages away from the waiting-room, where the constable and two plainclothes detectives were now with Quist, who would be charged before a special afternoon hearing at the magistrate's court. "Brown says she's quite something to look at. He's getting some photographs – she has a lot taken; they're displayed in shop windows before she gives a demonstration. Small, fragile, very sweet type, I gather, almost platinum blonde."

Roger wasn't thinking about Sybil Henry.

The shock of arrest had stiffened rather than weakened Quist's resolve; he wouldn't talk about Henry now, at least until he'd been advised. Roger looked at the facts, without bias. Henry had some sort of an alibi, where Quist had none at all.

But Roger didn't like the situation. There were too many undercurrents he didn't understand.

When he reached the G.I.'s desk, by himself, Roger found several memos on it, as well as a little pile of photographs. He sat down. Only Eddie Day was there, deeply preoccupied, and working with the tip of his tongue pressed against those protruding teeth. Ibbetson was transcribing the report of what Quist had said, before arranging for Quist to be photographed. Quist's clothes had already been searched, but nothing in them helped.

Roger picked up one of the photographs, of a girl who looked really charming. There was freshness about her, a hint of a provocative smile. Here was a kind of dream-girl; mother's dream, father's dream, young man's dream. Sybil Henry. He reminded himself that she would look and feel very different when she heard about Quist. That was, if she was as much in love with Quist as reports seemed to make out. And if her father was deeply involved, too—

Roger put down the photographs, all stamped *Creem Beauty Preparations* on the back, and looked through the others – of Rose Jensen, Quist and Charles Henry. He went through some reports, including carefully prepared notes on Quist's background, too. Brown and Ibbetson between them were really doing a job.

Then Roger came upon the statement from the man named Theophilus Pegg.

Pegg was Rose Jensen's second cousin, he said. His wholesale business was to do with cartons, all manner of cardboard boxes and cardboard packing, such as tubes. It had been established for twelve years, he had a sound reputation, his statement was quoted briefly and there was a note pinned to the report: *"Mr. Theophilus Pegg will be calling at 3.30 p.m. today."*

"Just send me one more good witness, and it can't go wrong," Roger mused. "Queer, though. If we could get hold of the altered cheques, or examine Cole's accounts and see if a large payment was credited at the relevant time, we'd get somewhere. Would Quist have talked of the altered cheques if he didn't think he could prove it? Would he have made up a story about a report to Gorringe?"

If Henry had taken the report away, it would be destroyed by now.

Roger stood up abruptly. "Well, a man must eat!" He lifted the telephone, told the operator he would be at the pub in Gannon Row, picked up his hat and jammed it on the back of his head, and went out. Few people were about. The usual sergeant and constable in the hall, the usual men at the foot of the steps, the others at the gate. Everything was quite normal.

The big dining-room of the pub was crowded, mostly with Yard men, but there were one or two journalists and a few local businessmen. Through a haze of smoke and the appetising smell of cooking, there was the sight of a dozen or so men tucking into their lunch, and more standing around the bar. Roger went to a long table where half-a-dozen others were sitting, including Superintendent Cortland, who he imagined would be one of the first to take advantage of the change of atmosphere at the Yard; for Cortland, the senior superintendent, had the ear of the A.C. Any gossip from him was worth thinking about.

"Hallo, Corty."

"Hallo, Handsome," Cortland said; that was friendly enough. "Having a cakewalk, aren't you?"

"Could be." '

The others at the table were laughing at some joke, and for a moment Cortland and Roger were not overheard. Cortland leaned forward, and said in a low-pitched voice: "Don't stand Jay up again; he didn't like it this morning."

Roger felt himself close up.

"Thanks," he said.

"Never knew how good Chatworth was until he'd gone," Cortland went on. "This chap will probably turn out all right, mind you. Bit of a red-tape-and-regulations type, that's the trouble; Chatworth was a bit careless in some ways. Okay." He leaned back as the others finished their huddle, and one called out to Roger; all that was quite normal, but Roger's feeling wasn't.

A waitress came up, absurdly small, with a black dress and a tiny white apron which seemed designed to emphasise her little pointed bosom. She had snappy blue eyes and far too much lipstick.

"Decided what you want yet, dear?"

"Is there steak pudding?"

"Always got what you want on, dear. Two veg?"

"Please."

"Anything to drink?"

"Half of bitter," Roger said.

"Okay, dear." The waitress went tapping off on absurdly high heels.

"What's the matter with you, Handsome?" one of the others said: "lost your thirst?"

Another quipped: "Chatworth must have taken it away with him."

It wasn't meant, but the attitude was apparent everywhere. The one essential thing was a swift success with this inquiry; at least that would give him an even chance with Jay, who could hardly ignore results. But there were complications he didn't begin to understand.

Roger was back at his desk at a quarter to three, and had hardly sat down before the telephone bell rang. He smoothed his hair and hesitated before picking up the receiver, then lifted it abruptly.

"West speaking."

"Ibbetson here," came the north-country voice with its unmistakable note of jubilation. "Glad you're back, sir; we've got the final nail for Quist's coffin."

Roger said slowly: "What is it?" He wanted it, and yet wasn't elated as he should be.

"We've found a kid who was in Page Street about nine o'clock on Monday. He says the chap on the bike went in to Number 31 soon afterwards. The kid's only sixteen, but he says he was hanging around hoping to see a girl." Ibbetson was elated enough. "He says it was the bike which interested him, and that's kid-like."

This was a six-inch nail.

"I'll see the boy after I've seen Pegg," Roger said. "It couldn't be better. I'm going over to the court now. You ready to leave?"

"Yes. Won't be long, will it?"

"Five minutes at the most; just formal evidence, that's all. If Saxby's are awake, their lawyer might ask for a remand, but it'll only be a formality. I'll see you downstairs, and we'll use my car."

In court he gave evidence of arrest, and applied for a remand in custody. Quist stood rigidly to attention in the dock during the brief hearing. When asked if he had anything to say, he said quite clearly: "I am not guilty, sir," and that was all. A youngish solicitor whom Roger recognised only vaguely made a formal "not guilty" plea. The magistrate remanded Quist in custody for eight days. Quist was about to leave the dock when something at the back of the court attracted his attention; he raised his hands as if in dismay, closed his eyes for a moment, and then stared at someone who had just come in.

Roger turned quickly, to see.

This was Sybil Henry, as fresh and charming as her pictures made out, yet looking lost and even bewildered. The youngish man joined her.

Quist was led out of court.

The girl said: "Where *is* he?" in a clear voice, as the few people in the public seats drifted out, and clearly she didn't mean Quist. She saw Roger. "Isn't that him?" She came hurrying, with the young solicitor behind her, clutching at her shoulder as if in protest. "Aren't you Chief Inspector West?"

"That's right," said Roger. "Can I help you?"

"Miss Henry," the youngish man interrupted, "if you say a word before consulting us, you may prejudice all Mr. Quist's chances of establishing his innocence. Please be advised by me."

Chapter Eight

Nails

The man was quite right.

If the girl knew anything which could help Quist, it would be best kept away from the police until the lawyers decided when to use her evidence. But if she could be made to talk, what she said might be used as another nail. Roger's job was to use every item of proof he could get.

"You'll never do any harm by telling the truth, Miss Henry," he said. "If you have any statement to make, I'll be glad to hear it."

"Miss Henry, I must insist—"

He might be a good solicitor, but the youngish man didn't know how to handle spirited young women. The glint in this girl's clear blue eyes told Roger that, and the other must have realised that he hadn't done very well. His lips were set tight in annoyance.

"How can you help?" Roger asked, in his most pleasant way. "We have only one purpose in mind, Miss Henry: to establish the truth. If Mr. Quist didn't—"

"He didn't!"

"Are you sure?"

"Of course I am."

"Were you with him all Monday evening?"

"Nearly—nearly all; he—"

Roger saw an elderly man saunter up, and was wary. He knew this man Samuelson, whose knowledge of the law was as detailed as that of any solicitor's, although he had no qualifications. He had been known to hover behind the scenes of many a big-case defence, his task to bend the law wherever it would bend. He had silvery hair, a charming smile and a pleasing voice. He also had the ear of many people of importance, and was reputed to be adviser on many financial matters to large business houses.

"Good afternoon, Chief Inspector. So we meet again." He sounded as if he was delighted. "In trying circumstances for Mr. Quist, of course, but I don't think we need worry about that too much. I'm holding a watching brief for Saxby's, by the way. But how are you?"

"Fine, thanks," Roger said. "Miss Henry—"

"If Miss Henry wants to say anything to help Mr. Quist, I hope she won't hesitate," said Samuelson, and his smile became even more charming. "True, in a lifetime of such work I've learned that it's wise to be carefully instructed in what one says to the police; the law can be used in such a variety of ways which the police know well – don't you, Chief Inspector? – and the layman knows very little. But if you're really anxious to make a statement now, Miss Henry, I'm sure the Chief Inspector would find time. I'd rather you made an appointment for later in the day, but—" He left the sentence in the air.

The young solicitor mopped his forehead.

"I—I would like to say something," the girl said in a low-pitched voice, "but perhaps it would—it would keep. Can you see me at once, Mr. Samuelson?"

So she knew him.

"I can, and I know the Chief Inspector will fit in an appointment to suit you at any time."

"Whenever you like," Roger promised, and his expression hid his disappointment. "Don't make it too late, will you?" He nodded, turned away, and went out of the court.

Samuelson could get away with murder.

Odd thought.

Quist was already on his way to Cannon Row, and would stay there for the rest of the day, then be taken to Brixton. Roger had

Theophilus Pegg to see, then the schoolboy, Clive Harrison. When both statements were signed and added to Mrs. Kimmeridge's, the defence would need an earthquake to shake the case, Samuelson or no Samuelson.

Roger didn't like Theophilus Pegg.

He didn't like rather fat, short, bouncy little men who drank too much, if their complexion and veinous nose were an indication, who talked too much, and who were anxious to make it apparent that they knew everything better than anyone else. But Pegg's statement was lucid, and he didn't seem to be a man who would be easily shaken. Questioned about his second cousin's statement that the friend 'Mike' had been jealous, he wouldn't shift. That's what she had told him, and that's what he would say in court if he were wanted as a witness. He hoped that if he was, he wouldn't have to waste a lot of time at the Old Bailey; he was a busy man, expanding business, couldn't get sufficient help, wanted every minute he could get for work. In future, for instance, would it be possible for the police to visit him, instead of his visiting the police?

"If we have cause for another interview, certainly," Roger said briskly. "Do you know Mrs. Kimmeridge, Mr. Pegg?"

"Met her. Downstairs flat at Page Street."

"That's right. Was your cousin on good terms with her?"

"Couldn't say," replied Pegg. "Kept herself to herself, Rose did. Neighbours pry. She didn't like prying. Can't see how it affects the issue. Fact is, my cousin was cruelly murdered." He made it sound like 'crooly'. "Want to find the swine."

"Would you recognise him again?"

"Said so *four* times this morning."

"We have to be doubly sure of these things, particularly on serious cases," Roger said, and pushed a dozen photographs, placed one on top of the other, towards the bouncy man. "Would you mind telling me if you have seen any of those people before?"

Pegg nodded, turned over photograph after photograph without giving them a second glance, and then came to Quist's, which was near the bottom. He stopped immediately, took the photograph between his flat thumb and flatter forefinger, and flicked it on to the desk.

"That's him. That's the man she called Mike. Saw him at her flat; called to get a document signed, didn't know she had company. Next time, at the Angel, Chelsea. You know it?"

"I've heard of it," Roger said.

The Angel was a big and popular pub, and it wouldn't be easy to get corroborative evidence, but it would have to be tried. Roger made a note to tell Ibbetson to go there himself, or to send a really good man, and quickly got rid of Mr. Theophilus Bouncy Pegg. He gave himself five minutes to check over what the man had said and to make notes, and then sent for the sixteen-year-old schoolboy who had seen Quist – or seen a man answering Quist's description – come out of the house in Page Street.

Oddly, Roger didn't really take to Clive Harrison, either.

The boy was polite. He stood almost to attention, saying he would rather stand than sit. He held his cap firmly in his hand, and he met Roger's eye, and yet – if this was a friend of his two sons, Roger would be a little wary of him, and want to know more before he encouraged the friendship.

But the boy repeated what he had told Ibbetson almost word for word, and picked out Quist's photograph almost as quickly as Theophiius Pegg had.

"So we've got Quist nailed in," Cortland said, about six o'clock that evening.

"Looks like it," Roger agreed. "What would you advise – that I just hand in my written report to the Assistant Commissioner, or present it in person?"

"Hand it to Miss Foster," advised Cortland. "Don't give him any excuse to say you're being too forceful. Didn't know him at all before he came here, did you?" Cortland was a big, powerful, shaggy and dark-haired man, with a perpetual frown.

"No."

"Not done anything to rub him up the wrong way?"

"Not that I can recall."

"Funny thing; he seems to have made a dead set at you," said Cortland. "Keep this to yourself, but he sent for your file this afternoon, wanted all details of the cases you've worked on, record of success and failure – all that kind of thing. He hasn't done that with anyone else."

Roger made himself grin.

"Why pick on me?"

Cortland was a humourless man, and except where his work was concerned, as tactless as an angry bull.

"Looked round for someone to make an example of, I suppose, and you seemed right. It's like being back in the ruddy army."

Roger ejaculated: "Back?"

Cortland grinned. "Did my seven years before I joined the Force, didn't you know? Sergeant-major before I finished. Ruddy terror, I was. I know all about coves like Colonel Uppity Jay; never satisfied until they've shown how strong they are, and let you know who's boss. What did we have to have one of them for?"

"Perhaps we were getting slack."

"Got you wondering about that, too, has he?" asked Cortland, and relaxed and patted the papers in front of him. "Forget it, Handsome. When's he got this one on a plate he'll look round for someone else. Perfect job, this is, and you haven't lost a second. How's he to know it's a typical West job? Could be a flash, in the pan, but it's a pretty bright flash. Okay, Handsome, your luck's in as usual!"

Roger took the written report along to the A.C.'s office. He caught Miss Foster preening herself in front of a mirror, and that didn't please her. He was formal, she was almost curt. There had been a time when he had been absolutely at home in this room; now it was like foreign territory.

"Good night, Miss Foster."

"Good night."

Little bitch.

He wondered if she used *Creem*, grinned wryly, and went back to his office. Eddie Day was still there, but everyone else had gone home. A dozen memos were on Roger's desk, mostly to do with cases which he had handed over earlier in the day. Ibbetson had left a note to say that he wasn't going to the Chelsea pub himself, as he was known there; he was sending a detective officer who lived at Hampstead and had just come from the Division. He would be armed with photographs of Quist and Rose Jensen.

There was also another report on Rose Jensen, although, it didn't say much. There was no particular reason why it should, but Roger wanted a clear picture. She might have been a married woman separated from her husband, thus explaining the wedding-ring callouses. She might have been divorced. She might have been widowed. She had come out of nowhere and taken this flat, and from then on had kept open house, as it were, for the men friends.

That couldn't have been too ostentatious, or more neighbours would have protested.

It was after seven before Roger cleared the desk. There was no word from the solicitor or Samuelson, and it wasn't likely that Sybil Henry was coming now. Samuelson had quietened her most effectively. Was that good or bad? Roger pondered as he left the Yard and walked briskly across to Cannon Row police station, where the constable on duty greeted him heartily; so did the C.I. in charge.

"Come for a word with Quist, Handsome?"

"Yes. How is he?"

"Taking it pretty hard."

"Solicitor been to see him?"

"Spent an hour and a half. Mr. Greenways."

"Right, thanks," said Roger, and went along to the cells. He walked briskly, with a sergeant behind him, and there was no doubt that Quist knew that he was there; but Quist was sitting sideways to the cell door, which was of iron bars, and didn't trouble to look round. He was reading an evening newspaper in a 'cell' as comfortable as many a bedsitter.

"They'll be over from Brixton at eight o'clock," the sergeant said.

"Good; thanks." Roger hesitated, not certain whether to speak to the accused man, who was so deliberately avoiding him, or whether to let Quist remain sullen.

"Quist."

Quist put the newspaper down slowly and looked round. He didn't speak. He hadn't much colour, and his shiny, red-rimmed eyes suggested that he had a severe headache. But there was a natural courtesy in the man, and now that the ice was broken he stood up slowly.

"Good evening."

"Got everything you need?"

"Yes, thanks."

"You'll be transferred to Brixton in an hour's time, but you'll find things pretty much the same there as they are here. I'll be ready to come and see you if you want to make a statement at any time."

"I've nothing more to say," Quist said, "except that I didn't know this woman Jensen and I didn't go into the house."

Why should Mrs. Kimmeridge lie?

Why should Theophilus Pegg lie?

Above all, why should a schoolboy lie?

One witness could be doubted, but three – it wasn't sensible to doubt them. Quist must be lying. Undoubtedly the solicitor, advised by Samuelson, had told him not to make any statement, except to keep reiterating his innocence, keep maintaining his lie. It was almost certain that Samuelson would use private inquiry agents, and probably it wouldn't be long before he discovered the names of one or more of the witnesses.

Why had Saxby's used Samuelson?

Roger put in a call to the chief of the Fraud Squad, whose deputy answered.

"No, nothing known against Cole's or any of the other firms you named," the deputy said. "They're all small businesses, run privately, not limited liability – and we're checking on the proprietors. But you know as well as I do that the name on the note-paper is often a stooge. It'll take us a day or two to find. We could work quicker if we could get our hands on those altered cheques."

"According to Quist, he enclosed them with a report that's now missing," Roger said.

"That keeps us from making a direct approach unless Saxby's make a formal complaint," the deputy declared. "I'll tell you what, though; Saxby's won't miss anything."

"What makes you so sure?"

"They've been using Samuelson for some time," the Fraud Squad man said. "He did one or two probes of this kind for big firms being defrauded. He's handy if a thing is to be hushed up."

"Ah," said Roger. "Thanks."

Roger saw the little grey Austin standing outside his house in Bell Street, Chelsea, when he reached home at a quarter to eight. He knew no one who owned a car like it. Few people were about, the neighbours would be in their back gardens or at their television sets. The antennae of dozens of sets were angled darkly against the pale blue of the evening sky. It was cooler than it had been for several days. Roger pulled into the drive-way, but didn't garage the car. He heard nothing as he approached the front door, and was a little puzzled. Usually one or the other of his sons was on the lookout for him, and he had telephoned his wife to say that he was leaving for home.

He caught a glimpse of slim, crossed ankles in the front, best, room; ankles he didn't recognise. Visitors? He let himself in with the key, and was startled to see his elder son, Martin – called Scoopy – standing just outside the front-room door, and peering into the room. Martin could see in but not be seen. He flushed bright red when he saw Roger, and stood as if caught out in some crime. He was very tall for his fourteen years, already five feet nine, and was broad and strong in comparison. He had a wide face, with even, attractive features.

"Hal—hallo, Dad," he whispered.

Roger didn't catch on.

"Hallo, Scoop," he said. "Who's there?"

The boy shook his head vigorously, and it was then that Roger understood. The visitor was quite something to look at, and at fourteen, Scoopy—

Roger moved swiftly, finger to his lips. Scoopy gave a half-hearted smile. Roger peered through a crack in the door, and then turned his head and nodded. That took a lot of doing, he was so startled by what he saw; but this wasn't a time to make the boy feel foolish.

"Nice, isn't she?" he whispered.

Scoopy nodded.

"Who?"

"She's a Miss Henry, or something. I heard her tell Mum. Mum had to go across to Mrs. Hallam's; something's up, and Richard's out with a crowd of the chaps. I—I'm doing homework."

Roger grinned, now.

Scoopy chuckled.

"All right," Roger said, still whispering. "Why don't you tap at the door when I've gone past, go in and keep her company until I come? Say I won't be a minute."

Scoopy's eyes brightened. "May I?"

"She won't bite!"

"I know *that*."

Roger went on to the living-room and the kitchen. He could do with a drink, but decided not to have one yet. He sluiced his face in stinging cold water, ran a comb through his hair and then went into the front room, where Scoopy was talking with surprising freedom.

"Well, you see, there's only a year's difference between my brother and me, hardly a year really, but I seem to grow in every way, and he's about average, so I look much older. That photograph gives you a good idea; it was only taken last year. And that's my mother, and that's my father; he's a very well known officer at Scotland Yard."

"Yes, I know," said Sybil Henry, and Roger gave her full marks for composure. "I've come to see him about a friend of mine who's suspected of a crime. Do you think he'll be willing to help if he can?"

"And I can tell you one thing," Scoopy said with the earnestness of his age, "if your friend didn't do it, he's quite safe with my father. The last thing he'd ever want is to find an innocent man guilty. That's certain."

"It's a great relief."

Roger's smile was twisted as he moved nearer the door, making some noise so that the others knew he was coming. He wondered if Samuelson knew that the girl was here.

Chapter Nine

Truth?

Roger went in.

Scoopy moved round quickly, still a little embarrassed, and the girl stood up. She had something of Quist's look about the eyes, one which it would be easy to believe was transparent honesty. She was everything her photograph promised, too. Roger didn't know why, but he hadn't expected her to have so good a figure; the line of her breast was quite lovely.

"I'll pop upstairs and get some work done," Scoopy said. "Good night, Miss Henry."

"Good night, Martin," she said, and held out her hand. Scoopy smiled with sudden embarrassment, touched her hand and vanished. Roger had a kind of preview, of the boy and a girl; Scoopy was already inches taller than Sybil Henry.

The picture faded with the smile on the girl's face. She kept up appearances until this moment, but suddenly her distress and anxiety showed clearly, and she was less sure of herself. Roger shook hands, and asked: "What will you have to drink?"

She hadn't expected that. "Oh. May I—may I have a gin and tonic? Or gin and something, anything."

"Of course." There was tonic water. He poured her drink and a whisky-and-soda for himself, sat on the arm of one armchair as she sat in another, opposite; already she was a little more at her ease.

Roger's eyes smiled.

"Here's to the truth!"

"The truth," she echoed, in a moment of sheer relief; she certainly had not expected him to behave like this. "Mr. West, I'm really sorry that I've worried you at home, but I didn't want to come to your office. I—" She had been speaking too quickly, and now paused, but Roger didn't prompt her. "The truth is that Mr. Samuelson and Mr. Greenways didn't want me to see you. I think I know why. I think they believe that I'm lying in order to try to help Mick."

This would make Samuelson's face red!

"Do they?"

"Mr. West," the girl said, "I've no idea what evidence you think you have, but I'm quite sure that Michael Quist did not kill that woman. It was sheer accident that he ever went to Page Street, and entirely my fault. I'm quite serious. Has—has Mick told you why he went there?"

She was fresh and attractive, charming and quite a girl to look at – and perhaps she was smart, too. Certainly Samuelson was. He could have sent her along, feigning sweet innocence, to try to learn one or two essential facts. If anyone would tempt a policeman to be indiscreet, a girl of this kind would.

"Mr. Quist has made a statement," Roger replied, "but of course I can't go into details."

Sybil seemed to be trying to read his thoughts.

"I suppose not," she said slowly, "and I'll have to take a chance and tell you exactly what happened the night before last. It really began with my father. He has been very strange and different in the past few weeks, without giving any explanation. The night before last he had a telephone call, and went out soon afterwards. Mother was very upset – there had been a quarrel just before he went out. I wish to heaven I'd never thought of it, but I asked Mick to follow father and try to find out where he went. I thought it was to see another woman, but wanted to be sure."

She didn't know that Roger already knew about this, and he didn't show how much this corroboration of part of Quist's statement interested him.

"Mick came back about ten o'clock," Sybil went on. "He had followed father to a house in Elwell – he didn't tell me the name of the street. He'd seen father with another woman, and his description of the woman was very like that of this Rose Jensen. He came back, and told me."

Sybil Henry stopped.

Roger took out cigarettes.

Thrown at a jury by the defence, this girl was enough to swing them right round in Michael Quist's favour. Samuelson and the others would want to keep her back if they could. After the girl had testified, the defence would almost certainly claim mistaken identity about the man seen going into and coming out of Rose Jensen's flat. That curious pro-Quist feeling made Roger examine his own attitude closely; and also the facts as known. He had swift mind-pictures of the three witnesses for the prosecution. Mrs. Kimmeridge, who would create a very good impression in spite of being garrulous; Theophilus Pegg, whom no one would like, but whose testimony would probably appear to be unshakeable, and the schoolboy, whom Roger hadn't really taken to.

Could three people make the same *mistake*?

"That's the simple truth," Sybil Henry said. "I can't help what others advise, Mr. West. I had to tell you. I'm positive that it is true."

"What time did your father get back?" Roger asked.

She knew exactly what he was driving at; couldn't have had a moment's doubt about it. She was switching suspicion from Quist to her father; in a case of divided loyalties, she had chosen to champion Quist.

Certainly she had tried to open up a new field of investigation.

"I suppose you think I've betrayed my father," she said, in a quiet voice.

Roger stood up, briskly.

"I don't think anything of the kind, Miss Henry. The chief trouble that we have with witnesses is their tendency to tell only part of the truth. What time did your father get back that night?"

"About eleven o'clock."

"How did he seem?"

She hesitated, and he half expected her to say that Henry had looked sick, or ill, or shocked or furtive. Then she surprised him.

"As a matter of fact, he seemed much more cheerful than before he'd gone out, as if something had happened to please him. He'd had a few drinks, I think. I know what it looks like, Mr. West, but I can't believe that he would behave like that if he had killed the woman. I think you have to look for someone else – other than my father and Michael."

"You could be right," Roger said non-committally. "Are you prepared to swear to this story in court?"

"Of course."

"You know there's been an eight-day remand, don't you?" Roger said. "There'll be a longer hearing a week tomorrow, when the magistrate will decide whether to dismiss the charge or to commit Mr. Quist for trial. Evidence given at that hearing can have an important bearing."

"I still hope you'll have to admit that it wasn't Michael, and withdraw the charge," Sybil said quietly. "You will try to establish the truth of what I've said, won't you?"

"I certainly will," said Roger. "All right, Miss Henry. Tell me everything that might help, and I'll check very thoroughly indeed."

"Thank you *very* much."

The telephone bell rang before she began.

There was an extension near Roger's chair. He moved across and picked it up. It was an even chance that this was someone from the Yard; if it wasn't, it would almost certainly be a friend of his wife.

"Roger West speaking."

"Good evening, Mr. West." The smooth voice of the speaker was vaguely familiar. "Will you be good enough to ask Miss Henry to speak to me?"

Now Roger placed him; this was Samuelson.

And this was a moment to be very, very wary.

"I know she is there," Samuelson went on, still smoothly. "I hope you understand that she is a very important defence witness, Mr. West, and that anything which might be construed into an attempt by the police to prejudice her evidence might have a most unfortunate effect."

The girl was pretending interest in a shelf laden with books, and could have no idea that this call affected her.

Could she?

"Mr. West—" tartness put an edge to Samuelson's voice.

"You do understand that any attempt to persuade a witness to withhold material evidence wouldn't do anyone any good, don't you?" said Roger, quite briskly. "I'll ask Miss Henry if she would like to speak to you. Hold on, please." He put the receiver against his chest, as the girl looked at him, as if startled. "It's Mr. Samuelson."

"But how on earth does he know I'm here?"

"That isn't important now – would you like to speak to him?"

She hesitated.

"He can't compel you to do what he wants," Roger said; "you're a completely free agent. But if I were you I'd hear what he has to say."

After a pause, Sybil said: "Yes, all right," and stood up and moved towards Roger. He handed her the receiver and moved away. He could guess what Samuelson was saying, but that wasn't his main preoccupation. His retort about persuading a witness to withhold evidence wouldn't put Samuelson off his stroke, but a complaint from Samuelson that his, Roger's, methods had been irregular could do a lot of harm. It was just the kind of thing that Jay would jump at.

Sybil Henry said: "I've made my decision, Mr. Samuelson, and I intend to stand by it, I'm sorry. Good night."

She rang off.

She could be decisive even if she did look fragile.

Roger felt more than ever aware that he must be very careful what leads he gave her. If he was accused of trying to influence witnesses …

"Mr. Samuelson just said that I mustn't tell you what I have already told you," Sybil said. "Mr. West, you will do everything you can to check what I've said, won't you?"

"I've already promised that I will. How long has your father had this worry?" Roger asked quickly.

"About three months."

"Had you any particular reason to believe it was another woman?"

"Not at first. I didn't realise that mother was really worried. She was afraid it was something at the bank."

"As far as you know, is everything all right there?"

"Yes."

"Have you ever seen any evidence that your father was conducting an affair? Lipstick on his clothes, for instance, perfume, powder – anything like that?"

"No."

"Would you know if your mother had seen any such thing?"

"I think so. I'm sure she didn't dream it was another woman."

"Has your father any close friends, who might be in his confidence about his *affaire*?"

"I don't think so," Sybil said hesitantly. "He hasn't many friends, and the bank dislikes scandal or anything remotely like that, so he wouldn't be likely to confide in anyone there."

"I see. Have you told your mother about this?"

She exclaimed: "Oh, no! Surely you won't have to—"

"I won't unless it's forced on me," Roger promised. "Now, while you're here – is there anything else you'd like to ask me?"

"I don't think so." Obviously Sybil was still worried by the last question, and she hesitated. "Mr. West, I don't want my mother harassed if it's at all possible to avoid it."

"And she won't be," Roger promised.

There was a ring at the front-door bell, and almost immediately a scraping of a chair upstairs; Scoopy's room was immediately above their heads. Roger was puzzled by the ring. This was a front room, yet he'd seen no car and heard no footsteps. He glanced across at the three casement-type windows, and saw that two were open, one of them near the front porch. It was just possible that someone had been listening there, and had decided to call.

Scoopy came hurrying downstairs.

The girl was standing up, looking a little puzzled, as if she couldn't understand what had distracted Roger.

The front door opened, and Scoopy said in his most courteous voice, as to a stranger: "Good evening, sir."

A man asked abruptly: "Mr. West in?"

"Yes, I think so." Scoopy spoke very slowly, as he always did if anything happened that he didn't understand or didn't like. "Will you wait just a minute? And what name, please?"

"He won't know me," the man said in the same abrupt way, and then his voice rose. "Get out of my way, you young brute." There was a brief pause, then what sounded like a scuffle.

Roger bounded towards the door, opened it and jumped into the passage.

Scoopy was reeling against the wall, and a man half a head taller and very broad and powerful was much nearer this door, his heavy features set angrily.

Roger barked: "What the devil's this?"

"If you don't teach that kid of yours some manners he'll get himself into trouble," the stranger rasped. "You think yourself pretty good, don't you, West? It's time you were taken down a few pegs. What with intimidating witnesses and teaching your son to attack—"

Scoopy was ashen pale with anger.

"Dad, I didn't do a thing. I just asked politely—"

"... little liar," the man said viciously; "if you're not careful I'll have him up in court for assault and battery. Where's Miss Henry?" He thrust his face close to Roger's and sneered: "I know she's still here; the car's outside. Trying to make her on the side? I noticed your wife's out, and with your own kid upstairs you ought to be—"

Roger cracked his fist against the man's jaw. As he did so, he saw the other grin, as if that was exactly what he had wanted to happen.

Two other men appeared, on the porch.

Chapter Ten

Photographs

"You saw him, didn't you?" the first man exclaimed, "I just asked if I could see Miss Henry, and he took a punch at me. Why, we ought to break his neck! "

"Why don't we?" one of the others sneered.

Roger had drawn back, slowly. He didn't understand everything, but he understood a lot. They were here to bait him, to establish the 'fact' that he had attempted to prevent them from seeing Sybil Henry. That was as far as he got; and for the moment it was as far as he needed to know.

He said, "Now get out, and hurry."

The two men behind the first crowded the doorway. Scoopy was nearer them, still flattened against the wall, very pale, with his eyes glittering.

"The Henry girl's here," the first man sneered. "It's time you stopped thinking you can throw your weight about, West, you've had it."

One of the others pushed forward, and in doing so, poked his elbow in Scoopy's chest. Scoopy drew his arm up, and the man spun round on him, vicious and angry, and slapped him across the face with the flat of his hand.

"Don't you raise your fist at me."

"Why, you rotten liar!" Scoopy breathed. "You tried to push me out of the way."

The man cried: "Call me a liar, would you? Why, I'll smack you down so—"

He drove his fist at Scoopy's stomach, while the man in front of Roger barred his path. Until that moment there was no doubt that everything had gone according to the callers' plans. It was the last moment, for the punch aimed at Scoopy's stomach didn't land. Scoopy wriggled, pushed the fist aside, and the man's knuckles cracked against the wall. There was a moment of shocked surprise, but the man had no chance to recover before Scoopy went for him savagely, arms working like pistons, cracking him on the jaw, the forehead and the nose.

The man nearer Roger spun round to join in.

"That's plenty from you," Roger said, and grabbed his arm.

He put all his strength into a blow at the other's stomach, and felt his fist bury itself in the flesh, for the man hadn't stiffened his muscles. The victim made a retching sound and staggered back, while the two men behind him were moving away almost desperately, and Scoopy was driving forward as if he wanted to kill.

"That's enough, Scoop!" Roger jumped forward. "Don't do anything else, or—"

Then several things seemed to happen at once. Sybil Henry came just behind Roger. Richard, his younger son, came tearing across the road from a neighbour's house. Janet, his wife, called out in alarm from across the street, and also came running. One of the three callers was already scurrying away from the house, and Scoopy's first victim followed him; there was only the man who had started the fracas.

"Oo, Scoop, what's up?" Richard cried excitedly. "Oo, I wish I'd been here!" He stormed the porch as the first man turned and started to run. "Oh, no, you don't!" cried Richard, and planted his six stone squarely in front of the man, who dwarfed him.

"Look out, Fish!" Roger cried.

"*Richard!*" screamed Janet.

The man swept his arm up. Richard, seeing the blow coming, ducked and went for the other's legs, but wasn't quite quick enough. The blow sent him staggering across the garden. The man went running on, and further along Bell Street the engine of a car started up. Roger, looking along, over hedges and past trees and shrubs, saw the top of the car and one man getting in.

Scoopy was racing after the third man.

"Scoopy!" cried Janet wildly, and blocked his path. "What's the matter with you all? Have you gone mad?"

Scoopy stopped. The running man reached the car and climbed in, and the car started off, its engine roaring.

"I simply don't understand it," Janet West said helplessly.

They were in the kitchen, twenty minutes later, with the front door closed and the last of the curious neighbours gone, although some of the boys' friends were still outside, all agog. Sybil Henry had insisted on driving away at once; she had seemed almost distraught. Roger had telephoned the Yard, and arranged for her to be followed home.

"Why on earth should they come here and pick a fight?" demanded Janet.

"Well, I don't know why they should, but they did," said Scoopy feelingly. "I was never more surprised in my life." He was feeling his knuckles gingerly.

"I can't leave the house for half an hour without *this* happening," said Janet, recklessly. She looked strikingly attractive, her eyes very bright because of what had happened, her cheeks flushed and her dark hair ruffled, with its clusters of loose curls. She wore a navy-blue dress with white cuffs at the sleeves and a white collar. "Roger, who was that girl? What has been happening?"

"Go on, Dad, tell us," urged Richard. His cheek was a little flushed from the buffet, and the red made his eyes look a startled blue.

"Can I trust you boys not to say a word about this?" Roger asked, very quietly. "If you promise to keep it absolutely to yourself, I'll tell you why I think it happened."

Something in his expression silenced Janet, who was obviously as curious as the boys.

"I won't talk," Scoopy said.

"I promise," Richard said very earnestly.

"Right, then! This is how it goes. The young lady was Miss Henry, a witness in a case which I'm investigating. She came to see me against the wishes of her adviser. It was important to him that she shouldn't talk to me privately. As she did, in order to discredit me, the adviser sent those men. He—"

"But why?"

"Wait for it," Roger went on briskly. "He wants to make it appear as if I was interviewing Miss Henry against her will. He sent three men to protest against this, and to pick a quarrel. Those three men will be prepared to swear that we started the trouble by refusing to let the first man talk to Miss Henry."

Richard's eyes looked huge as he tried to grasp the implications.

"Why, it's disgusting," Scoopy said at last. "They're not even honest!"

"You'll soon put them in their place," declared Richard. "You'll have them up for salt and battery, won't you?"

"For what?" asked Janet weakly.

"Salt and bat—"

"*Ass*ault and battery," Scoopy said, in lordly, patronising tones, "not salt, you ass, *ass*—" He saw the pun, and broke off to chuckle.

"We'll fix 'em all right," Roger said bluffly. "Now, that's everything for tonight. I'll tell you of any developments later. If either of you breathes a word of this, you could spoil my answer to the accusations, and make it deuced awkward, so watch yourselves."

"We've promised," Scoopy said simply.

"Well, I suppose you know what you're doing," Janet said, looking worriedly at Roger. Then she moved briskly towards the larder. "But you must be famished. I've a salad and some veal-and-ham pie. If you want a sandwich or anything, boys, you'll have to get it yourself …"

"What are you doing to do?" Janet asked, when the boys had gone to bed. "Are you sure it was this Samuelson man?"

"Pretty sure, and as sure that I'll never get him for it," Roger said. He tried to hide his anxiety, but did not make much of a job of it, "I always knew Samuelson was a slippery customer, but I'm damned if

I can see what he's up to this time? Why go to these lengths to save Quist?"

He half expected the telephone to ring again, but it didn't. He went upstairs a little after midnight. Janet was getting into bed, wearing a pale pink nightdress with a low neckline and short sleeves. Almost for the first time since she had come in, Roger saw her just as Janet, his wife. He went across and kissed her.

"For forty, you're a living marvel!" he said.

"Thirty-nine. Roger, what is worrying you so much?"

"It's a damned queer business."

"Darling, I'm not asking you to tell me the intimate details of life at the Yard or about this particular case, but I can see that you're as jumpy as a cat, and a queer case doesn't usually do that to you. What is it? You seem to think the way these men came is a disaster."

"The all-seeing eyes," said Roger, and sat on the side of the bed. There were moments for simple truth. "The timing is the trouble. Colonel Jay has decided to demonstrate his supreme authority, and I'm picked out as the awful example, always too ready to take liberties. The Army does not like liberty-taking officers. If this scuffle is reported to Jay, he'll be predisposed towards believing the worst. Chatworth would have heard my side and brushed the other off, but Jay isn't going to. I think Samuelson's behind this, and I can't see Samuelson losing his chance of dropping poison. If Samuelson could get me off this case, it might help him, by suggesting a weakness that isn't there. That could be the motive behind it. If the Yard is in danger of being accused of trying to influence a witness, then there'll be a lot of trouble on that score alone. Jay's already the new broom. This will convince him that some really sharp bristles are needed."

He stopped, still nursing his knees.

Janet said slowly: "You're really badly worried, aren't you?"

"Yes, sweet, I am."

"There isn't a man on the Force who works like you do; why, you practically take your job to bed with you!" She stormed to his defence. "It's wickedly unfair."

"I'm just wondering if I did throw my weight about too much when Chatworth was there," said Roger slowly, "and whether there isn't a good case to be made out for Jay." There was a long pause. Then: "What an incredible man you are!" Janet said in a small voice. "You'll lean over backwards not to be unfair to the other man, no matter what he does to you. So far as I'm concerned, this Colonel Jay is a pompous old fool, and if he does anything to cramp your style, he's crazy. I tell you—no! Roger! Roger, dar ... No!"

Roger was at the Yard at half-past eight next morning. There were a few reports on his desk, but the mail hadn't been brought round yet, and nothing here was important. He assumed that he would have to see Jay at ten o'clock, and didn't intend to miss the appointment.

Ibbetson and Brown were early, too; and eager.

"I went over everything last night, and couldn't find a flaw," said Ibbetson. "Read the Hadworth Division report, and talked to the sergeant who'd double-checked at the Rose and Crown. With a bit of luck we'll have it all sewn up in the next week, and Quist committed for trial."

"We won't take anything for granted," Roger said flatly. "I'm not going into details, but I picked up a few odds and ends last night. I want you personally to check Division on Henry's movements on Monday night – keep it to yourself if you can. And try to find out if he was ever with Rose Jensen at that pub. Look for any indication that he knew the woman. Then check the Henry girl's story. Did Quist really go to Henry's place first and follow Henry? We've got to be positive." Roger was in full flood. "There's a thing I missed yesterday, too. I want Mrs. Kimmeridge to see either Henry or his photograph. If she identifies him as the older man with Rose Jensen on Monday, then we've got another job on our hands. If she doesn't, try the other neighbours who saw the older man. Got it all?"

"Right," said Ibbetson.

"Good. Brown, you get over to Saxby's. They may be difficult, but let that ride. Talk to all of Quist's friends, and to everyone in the office. We want to find out if he was having an *affaire* before the meeting with Miss Henry. I know what the woman who looks after his flat says, but she could be wrong. This *affaire* we're looking for would be an occasional visit to Rose Jensen, not infatuation or a real love affair, and it wouldn't necessarily have affected Quist's habits. Take two D.O.s with you, and try and get every job finished this morning. Get in touch with any friends Quist might have outside of Saxby's, too, particularly that tennis club. If you can pick up anything which suggests that he knew Rose Jensen or anyone like her, it will help."

"And if Charles Henry knew her—" Ibbetson began.

"We might swing towards him," Roger said. "All set?"

"Yes," they said, and hurried off.

Roger scowled at the door as it closed. It was a little before nine o'clock, and there was no hope of news from the two sergeants for an hour or more. If he'd had his way he would have seen Mrs. Kimmeridge himself, but the shadow of the Assistant Commissioner lay dark upon his desk.

The door opened swiftly.

Bill Sloan came in, big and boyish-looking, with his fresh complexion and his stiff, close-cut hair and a brown suit which looked a little too small and tight for him. He carried several newspapers, and made a bee-line for Roger.

"Morning, Bill. What's on your mind?"

"Roger, you seen the *Witness*?"

"No. What's in it?"

Sloan didn't speak, but unfolded a newspaper as he came towards Roger's desk. The *Witness* was one of the small picture-papers; it featured girls with plunge necklines, bulging bras and flesh-coloured skin-tight bathing-suits, and it throve on sensation. *Witness – the Paper Which Watches For the People* ran its slogan, set in a red shield on the front page. That front page was used either for the most eye-catching beauty, or for series pictures, others starring the *élite* who were caught up in divorce cases, telling of sensation picture by picture.

Even before Sloan reached the desk, Roger felt himself going cold. Then the other C.I. spread the *Witness*'s front page on his desk.

Here were eight pictures.

The first was a beauty, of Sybil Henry, and it showed her as charming as she really was.

The second was of him, Roger West, standing outside the Bell Street house with Janet and the boys; a picture taken several months ago.

Then came the action pictures: of Scoopy striking his assailant, of the general mêlée, of Sybil Henry standing and looking on, as if horrified. There followed two others, each of a man who had been at Bell Street last night; one had his nose patched with adhesive tape, the other had a bandage round his head and one eye hidden beneath a swathe of bandages.

The caption read:

> "Last night three *Witness* reporters called on Chief Inspector Roger 'Handsome' West of New Scotland Yard and asked to see a young lady, girl friend of a man charged with murder, and a vital witness for the defence. She was at Chief Inspector West's private home.
>
> "The *Witness* understands that the Chief Inspector refused their request and used violence to show that he meant business.
>
> "The *Witness* asks a simple question: Is this the way we people of a great democracy want our police to behave?"

Chapter Eleven

Roger Alone

"Well, they didn't lose much time over that," Roger said gruffly, and tried to get rid of the chilling effect of the story and the pictures. "I expect they made the A.C. a present of the *Witness* this morning, if they didn't send him prints of the photographs. Taken without flashlights, of course. Clever, isn't it?"

"What the hell happened?" Sloan demanded.

"I think Samuelson disliked it when Sybil Henry came to see me against his advice, and laid this on with the *Witness*. I'd stake half my pension that he knew there was a rift in the lute here; possibly knows that Jay is new-brooming, and saw his chance and took it. After this, I won't be allowed anywhere near Sybil Henry. I won't be allowed on the case at all." Roger put a cigarette to his lips, slowly: "If you were in Jay's position, what would you do?"

Sloan grunted: "It's the very devil!"

"What would you do?"

"I wouldn't have much choice. I'd take you off this case, even if I didn't suspend you from duty altogether."

"That's it," said Roger. "Suspend me from duty, and play right into Samuelson's hands. It looks as if Samuelson's decided that he can prove that the girl sent Quist after her father, and gave him a good, romantic reason for going. Samuelson wanted to spring that on us, and now he can't. So he hit back, and the *Witness* jumped at the chance. No, I don't see what Jay can do but take me off the job. Even

Chatworth would have a hell of a job to keep me in the clear." Roger was drawing very hard at the cigarette. "Bill, this case isn't what it seems. You followed it?"

"Pretty closely."

"Ever known me stick my neck right out?"

"Never known you not!" For the first time Sloan found a grin. "What's on your mind?"

"I've a lot to do, and I can't do it from the desk or from home," Roger said. "I'm going out on the job, and when Jay sends for me I won't be here. I doubt if he'll put a general call out for me, and I'll make sure that I'm not picked up by accident. And I'm—"

Sloan gripped his forearm, tightly.

"Don't be a fool, Roger! It's no use trying to keep out of Jay's way. He'd smack you down with a bang."

"Yes. Bill, listen. Either Sybil Henry came to Bell Street last night and lied to me, or some of the statements we've had from apparently reliable witnesses can't be trusted. But they're all corroborated, most of them three ways. Ibbetson's checking the girl's story. I want to check three witnesses: first Mrs. Kimmeridge; then Theophilus Pegg; then that boy, Clive Harrison. I want to find out if there's any possibility of collusion among them. If there is, and if they gave evidence and were believed – as they would be as things stand now – they could get an innocent man condemned."

"Getting yourself in deep trouble with Jay won't help."

"I've got to do one of two things: either work on this myself quickly, and get results, or else give a final report to Jay. I've got to tell him that I've a hunch that three – *three* – potential witnesses for the prosecution are lying, and ask him to try to prove it. He's going to hand the job over to another C.I. who will think I've gone crazy. In other words, it isn't going to get done."

Sloan said almost desperately: "I think you've gone crazy already. If you duck out, you'll be telling Jay that you don't give a damn for routine or for him. It'll be as good as telling him that you're going to tackle a job your way, or not at all."

"That's right."

"It's madness!"

"Supposing it's the only way? Supposing I believe that there's a real risk that Quist will go down for a job he didn't commit? What am I to do? Stand to attention, apologise for wanting to get the right man, take an enforced holiday? When I've been told that I'm not to work on the job, it would be deliberate indiscipline to do so. Until I have been told—"

The telephone rang on his desk.

It was twenty-five minutes past nine.

He hesitated; and then motioned to the instrument. Sloan gritted his teeth as he lifted it.

"Chief Inspector Sloan …"

He seemed to draw himself up to attention.

"Yes, sir."

He looked Roger straight in the eye.

"No, sir, he's not in the office … Yes, I'll tell him the moment he comes in. Goodbye, sir."

Sloan put the receiver down slowly, and didn't look away from Roger. Roger stubbed out his cigarette, very deliberately, and began to speak: "When Ibbetson and Brown get back, tell 'em to sit tight until they get instructions – they're not to do anything else for me; I don't want them, you or anyone else to be caught up in the backwash of this."

"Roger, you're a bloody fool."

"That's right."

"Where are you going?"

"Out," said Roger, and picked up his hat. He placed it jauntily on the back of his head, and went to the door. As he reached it, it opened and Eddie Day and Carter came in; and Carter had a copy of *Witness* in his hand. "'Morning, gentlemen," said Roger, and pulled the brim of his hat down over one eye. "Not so hot, is it?" He went out, leaving the others staring after him.

"'E gone haywire?" demanded Eddie Day.

"Perhaps he's always been like it," Carter said.

Sloan bit back a retort, and dropped into his chair.

There were several ways out of the Yard. Roger chose the gateway near Cannon Row, knowing that there was little chance that Jay, whose office was on the other side of the building, would see him. The officers at the gates saluted him as he drove out. He went straight to St. James's Park, where many cars were parked all day, found a space, and put his car into it. He locked it, and then took a taxi.

"Brixton jail," he said.

"Car broken down, Mr. West?" The cabby kept a straight face.

"No. I just daren't be recognised this morning," Roger said, and grinned. "I might get my picture in the papers."

The cabby's poker face vanished.

"You're a card, you are," he said. "Okay, Brixton." He drove in a U turn and went back across Parliament Square, turning over Westminster Bridge. Roger glanced back at the tall Yard buildings, one red, the others grey. They looked imposing against the clear blue of the sky. It was a perfect morning, and the bridge was crowded. He watched the crowd, but he was thinking hard and faster than he wanted; he might make mistakes through hurrying. He needed a car which wouldn't be easily recognised or placed, and it would be impossible to hire one without being recognised; after this morning's photographs, someone would be bound to notice him.

Did he need a car?

Or a taxi?

It took twenty minutes to reach the prison.

"Don't stay long," the cabby said, and grinned.

"How about waiting?" asked Roger, and soon convinced the man that he was serious. "Not here, though. Go round the corner, and keep your flag down. Don't tell anyone who you've got for a passenger, or you could run into trouble."

"Okay, Mr. West. I know when to keep me mouth shut."

"Do you have radio?"

"Owner driver, that's me; I'm not going to be at the beck and call of some little bit of skirt in an office."

"Fine," said Roger. "Stay with me, I might want you most of the day."

"Suits me," the cabby said. "In case you need to know, my name's Nobb."

"Old Nob?"

"Just Nobb."

"Right; thanks," said Roger, and got out.

Everything was normal at the prison; warders and policemen looked at him sideways, which was to be expected, but there was no hint that they'd had special instructions; if Jay went to those lengths, it would be much later in the day. No one was surprised when he asked to see Michael Quist, and the warder in charge of the remand cells said: "Didn't sleep much during the night, but dropped off this morning. He didn't wake up, and we left him."

"That's fine," said Roger. "I don't think he's one who needs it rough." He walked alongside the man, who took his keys off his belt; soon they reached Quist's cell, with its barred door.

Quist stood up eagerly from a small chair, but his disappointment was very clear when he recognised Roger. "Leave us, will you?" Roger said to the warder.

"Going to be long, sir?"

"Ten minutes at most."

"Okay." The warder stood aside, then closed the door behind them, and locked it. Of course, he had to; routine was routine, and risks were risks, but the locking of the door did something to Roger. If Jay did get a brainwave, if he did telephone an inquiry—

"Good morning," Quist said quietly.

He looked tired, but well; his colour was back, and the glint in his eyes was vividly remindful of Sybil Henry's. He was obviously wary.

"Good morning," Roger greeted, and offered cigarettes, then went on abruptly: "Quist, I saw Miss Henry last night. She told me her version of what happened on Monday. Give me yours again, quickly."

Quist said slowly: "You've no right to ask me to make a statement without my lawyer being present."

"I've every right, but I can't make you answer," Roger said. "You can shelter behind Samuelson or anyone you like. They're interested only in one thing: getting you free. They might be able to do it with an astute defence. They might quite easily get a 'Not Guilty' verdict which would leave a bad taste in your mouth and the public's mouth for a long time. They're not interested in finding out who did kill this woman, though. I am. I don't give a damn whether it was you, Miss Henry, or any one out of the nine million people in London, I want the truth and nothing else, because I don't want to take the slightest chance that a murderer is running around loose. I think you can help. If you didn't do this job, someone seems determined to make it look as if you did. So either you did it or you're being framed. Don't interrupt, just think. Why should anyone want to frame you? What else was in that report? What do you know that you haven't told me? You might give me the line I need to start looking for someone else. The one thing you have to believe is that I want the murderer in dock, not any particular individual."

He stopped.

He could not realise how tensely he had spoken, or how it impressed Quist. He did see the change in Quist's expression, as if this approach bewildered him. He knew that time was going fast, that there was the risk that Jay would pick up the telephone and check.

Quist said: "I've told you everything I can."

Chapter Twelve

Nobb

"Listen to me," Roger said almost desperately; "if you're innocent we need proof. You've got to try to remember every trifle that may help."

"I've made myself silly, thinking about it," Quist said helplessly.

"Do you know a man named Pegg – Theophilus Pegg?" Roger asked.

"I don't know him, but I know of him," Quist answered. "He's an agent for several box-making and packaging manufacturers and specialises in unusual box designs for tropical use. Saxby's do quite a lot of business with him."

"Were any Pegg cheques altered?"

"I didn't see any," said Quist, "but I'm only a junior member of the staff, and couldn't get the cancelled cheques or bank statements on my own authority. I couldn't ask Mr. Gorringe to send for them without saying why. I just watched when and where I could. I found cheques for Cole's, Edger's and Marshall's." Quist broke off, frowning, as if he had just remembered something. Roger waited.

"I'll tell you one thing I hadn't realised before," said Quist. "The invoices from Pegg's, Marshall's, Cole's and Edger's were all printed by the same people, and made out on the same typewriter – an old one. I suppose I noticed it but didn't give it a second thought. Could that help?"

"Possibly." Roger fought back excitement. "Did you say this in your report?"

"No."

"What made you write out the report after all?"

"A new cheque came in, altered by three hundred pounds."

"Whose cheque?"

"Cole's, the fuel people."

"Did anyone see you make out that report?"

"I don't see how they could; I did it at home."

"Do you think Henry had any reason to suspect you were watching him?"

"Well—I suppose he could have. I questioned him pretty closely when I last saw him, about smaller discrepancies, and his method of checking."

"So he could have suspected that you were on to him," Roger said. "What kind of envelope was the report in?"

"A thick manilla legal envelope."

"Addressed to Gorringe in your handwriting?"

"Yes; I put it in his *In* basket, and covered it with some file copies of letters. Mr. West, in view of that report, why was I charged?" Quist demanded.

Roger said. "Gorringe didn't get it."

Quist began: "What on earth—" and then stopped, backed away, and sat down heavily. His colour seemed to run from his cheeks.

"I see," he said after a pause. "No altered cheques, nothing to bear out what I've said. It's—but it's incredible! " He could see that it might be deadly.

Roger said quietly: "Get it into your head that we don't plan to convict innocent men. Now, I'd like some other details – of Saxby's business with these firms, for instance."

"Most of them supply fairly regular things – food, for the canteen; fuel; goods in steady use. Pegg's are different. We have our own air freight service to the tropics, and Pegg's do the boxing and packaging, and supply special packaging material."

"What kind of goods do Saxby's make for the tropical market?"

"Oh, everything in rubber and plastic, like hot-water bottles, stoppers, engine parts, soles and heels for shoes, what we call mechanical goods," Quist said. "They're mostly moulded, and it's a very big business."

"I see," said Roger. "Do you know Theophilus Pegg personally?"

"No."

"Do you know a boy named Clive Harrison?"

"I know a David Harrison, a George Harrison and a Marjorie."

"A sixteen-year-old schoolboy."

"No."

"A Mrs. Kimmeridge?"

"No. Who are —"

"Ever been to the Angel, in Chelsea?"

"Yes, years ago."

"Not this year?"

"Not for seven or eight years. I used to go to the Polytechnic at Chelsea, and—"

"All right. Had you any earlier idea of any trouble between Mr. and Mrs. Henry?"

"No, but I didn't know much about them. It didn't surprise me that Henry was on edge, of course. I thought he himself was probably altering the cheques under pressure." Quist seemed as frank as a man could be; as frank and honest as Sybil Henry. But if he was telling the truth, was the girl? Supposing Sybil Henry had deliberately sent Quist after her father, knowing that her father was going to kill the other woman. Quist would be the victim of a vicious, cruel conspiracy.

"Ever been into the branch of the bank where Henry works?" Roger asked.

"Yes, now and again, to pay money in."

"Ever heard any kind of money trouble in the Henry family?"

"No. I hope you aren't going to push these questions about them; I don't know that I want to."

"That's the lot," Roger said, with the briskness which had characterised him since he had come in the cell. "But I ought to add this. I can't use what you've told me, because there was no witness to either statement. You need not tell Samuelson that you've just talked to me. It's entirely up to you. But my own view is that it would be wise to tell him, and for you to stick to your statement, if it's true. Don't let him or anyone else stop you from making and signing it officially. Don't put it off."

Quist said: "I'll have to think it over, and do what seems wisest."

"I'm doing what I think best, too," Roger said, with a twisted smile.

The brightness of the sunshine outside the prison walls looked inviting. Roger stepped out, the big gates clanged behind him, and he found himself breathing deeply. There were so many things he wanted to do urgently – among them, see Mr. Bouncy Pegg again. The taxi was round the corner, and the driver had a copy of the *Witness* in front of him; but he made no comment, except: "So they didn't keep you in?"

"Not today," Roger said. "Now Chelsea, please: the Midpro Bank in the High Street near the Town Hall."

"Right."

They reached the bank at five minutes past ten. At ten minutes past Roger came out; he had a hundred pound notes distributed about his pockets, and hoped that they would be more than enough to meet any emergency. He went next to Hadworth Station, stopped there, went to a kiosk and telephoned Janet. She answered herself.

"Jan."

"Roger ! Have you seen —"

"Yes. Don't worry about it."

"But hasn't the Assistant—"

"Haven't seen him," Roger said. "I'm following a lead which might take me out of town for a day or two, so don't worry."

"A *day* or so?"

"Yes," Roger said. "Don't be too surprised if you don't hear from me. How did the boys like the pretty pictures?"

"I don't think they've seen them yet," Janet said, "but everyone else has. The telephone's been ringing about every five minutes."

"Tell 'em all the same – no comment," said Roger. "'Bye, my sweet."

But he doubted whether he had fooled her.

He went straight to Henry's bank, as nearly sure as he could be that Henry had known Rose Jensen, and knew much that he hadn't admitted. The bank was crowded, but a clerk recognised him, and said: "I'll let Mr. Henry know you're here, sir."

"Thanks," Roger said.

Henry kept him waiting for nearly ten minutes, and when Roger sat opposite him, there was a noticeable smell of whisky. So Henry had needed some Dutch courage.

Roger was brusque ...

Henry said flatly that he had never seen or heard of Rose Jensen and that it was unfortunate that his daughter had become enamoured of a man who had. He hadn't been to Page Street. He hadn't left the Rose and Crown. That was all. Yet he gave Roger an even stronger impression that he had a lot to hide.

Roger felt curiously dejected when he left the bank – and then came out of his reverie with shock. Ibbetson was walking across a zebra crossing, towards the bank; he might have a message from Jay.

Roger waited, tensely. Ibbetson hadn't caught sight of him, but the detective officer did now, and they both glanced his way. Then they drew up, a yard away from a zebra crossing, and it was still difficult to be sure whether they had any special message or not.

"Good morning, sir." That was the D.O.

"'Morning."

"Glad I've caught you, sir," said Ibbetson, and could not even begin to suspect how tightly Roger's teeth were clenching. "I knew you wanted quick results, so I went to the Hadworth *Echo* office. I felt sure they'd have one or two photographs of Mr. Charles Henry, and they had. I took them along to Mrs. Kimmeridge, with several other photographs. She didn't pick Henry out, sir, but said that she was sure that the old man who went to see Miss Jensen wasn't in any of the photographs."

Roger felt his heart thumping.

"Did you check with any other neighbours?"

"Two now say they've seen this fat chap at Page Street, but it didn't get us anywhere," Ibbetson said. "One didn't pick out any photo at all, the other picked out Henry and two others, but said she couldn't really be sure. The only person we can trace who's seen this chap at close quarters is Mrs. Kimmeridge, sir, and she's quite positive."

"I see," said Roger. "Well. Anything fresh about Henry at the Rose and Crown?"

"There's no doubt he was there until after ten o'clock. A barman says he was in early, too – a relief barman, who seems all right."

"Keep at it," Roger said. "Try to find out if Henry left at all, and the length of time he was away, if any." But it looked as if Henry was in the clear. "Anything new about Rose Jensen?"

"We have picked up a trifle." Ibbetson spoke almost as if he was deliberately making an understatement. "We found one or two envelopes addressed to her in the dustbin, but don't know who from. There was also a spoiled envelope which she'd started to address."

"Who to?" Roger asked eagerly.

"A Mrs. Harrison."

There was a long pause, while traffic and people passed, and thoughts jostled each other in Roger's head. At last he said: "No address?"

"No, sir. There was a big ink blot, which had spoiled the envelope."

"Harrison," Roger said heavily. "Well, it isn't exactly an unusual name. Do you remember the boy Harrison's address?"

"Yes, sir. 101 Hadworth Palace Road."

"Sure?"

"Positive. He goes to Hadworth Grammar School."

"Thanks," said Roger. He felt more doubtful about the case than ever. Ibbetson had dug out a cousin of Rose Jensen, who was the owner of a business connected with the forged cheques which Quist had talked about. Now, the dead woman was known to someone bearing the same name as a second witness against Quist. Coincidence?

At least nothing Ibbetson said suggested that either of the Yard men knew that he was being sought by Jay, but Roger wanted a word with Sloan or anyone who could tell him whether Jay was making much fuss.

Ibbetson and the other man went off.

Roger walked past the taxi, and said to Nobb: "Go round the next corner, then the first left. I'll join you in that street." He walked on after the man's grunt of acknowledgment, and reached a corner and turned round it, so that he would meet the cab. Ibbetson hadn't followed him. It was only two minutes before Nobb came up, and he got in.

"Do you know Page Street, Elwell?"

"Know *of* it," Nobb said.

"Take me there, wall you? And when we get into it, head for Hadworth Palace Road."

"Hadworth Palace? Why don't we go there first?"

"Don't you want the meter to keep ticking away?"

"Okay," the cabby said.

They reached Page Street at about a quarter to eleven. A policeman stood at one corner, another outside Number 31. Rose Jensen's flat was sealed now, but the police were making sure that sightseers didn't become a nuisance. Both policemen stared towards the cab, but it wasn't likely that they recognised Roger. The cab turned right at the end of the street, then doubled back for five minutes before turning off to Hadworth Palace Road.

Roger was drawing very deeply on a cigarette.

Clive Harrison had said that he had been waiting to see a girl. That girl might be worth an interview. He was anxious to see the boy again, and to get an assessment of him from someone quite dispassionate.

"Hadworth Grammar School, now," Roger said to Nobb. He tossed his cigarette out of the window, and sat back. He was getting used to the idea that he was on the run, but it wasn't remotely exhilarating. The need to know Jay's reaction nagged at him all the time.

The school was a modern one, built only on the ground-floor, with playing-fields on three sides. The tree-lined road was bright and shady in the warm sun. No houses were near the school, which stood on a slight rise of ground; there was a public park near it. Roger had the cabby stop outside the front entrance, and went hurrying towards it, still looking about him as if there was a risk of being seen by someone who might give him away.

The big, bare hall was empty, and Roger glanced into several doorways, but found only empty rooms. Then a little red-haired man came along, taking very short steps.

"Can I help you?"

"I'd like a word with the headmaster, please, if it's possible."

"I'll ask him, sir; I'm his secretary. This way, please."

It was possible.

The headmaster was not unlike Charles Henry to look at, except that he was ten years younger, much more grey and had unmistakable lines of humour at his eyes; Henry had looked as if he hadn't laughed for years. This room was spare and bright and somehow not quite right; a little shabby, perhaps. But the headmaster was an adept at putting callers at their ease.

"I don't think I've had the pleasure of meeting you, Mr. West, but your son—"

Roger broke in, smiling. "I'm sorry, I've probably misled you. My son isn't here. I've called about another boy."

"I assure you I haven't mistaken your identity," said the headmaster. "We had your elder son here only a few weeks ago, in the semi-finals of the boxing competition. We have a very fine gymnasium. Remarkable physique for a boy of his age. I—er—I almost felt sorry for his victim that night!"

Here at least was warmth and friendliness. "How can I help you, Mr. West?"

"I'd like a confidential report on one of your senior pupils," Roger said, "and I really mean confidential."

"Are you asking officially?"

He wasn't under suspension yet.

"Yes."

"Then of course I'll give you all the help I can."

"Thank you," said Roger, and put his question very clearly and deliberately: "Do you think it is wise to rely on the word of a pupil here named Clive Harrison? In your opinion, is he completely reliable and trustworthy?"

The headmaster's smile faded, and for a while he made no attempt to answer.

Chapter Thirteen

Angry Mother

The longer the headmaster sat there, the more Roger believed that even if he answered at all, he would be evasive; but evasion would be as good as an answer. The bare, shabby office with the gown and mortar-board hanging behind the flat desk, which needed re-varnishing, was very quiet until the headmaster said: "Clive is a remarkable boy in many ways, Mr. West. He is probably the most brilliant we have at the school – perhaps it would be more honest to say our one really brilliant boy. He is quite exceptional in his grasp of mathematics, and we all hope that he will go a long way. There's no doubt that he should. However, the school is only one factor in education, and not always the most important. Environment has a great deal to do with the making of a boy's future, and I can tell you this: Clive lost his father, in rather unhappy circumstances, only three years ago. Until that time his father had a very strong influence over him. Since then—well, I can say that he's headstrong, and whenever allowed to have his head, very difficult. I confess that I would very much like to help him. Frankly"—the headmaster waved his hands a little, and gave a taut smile—"I'm talking so freely because it is conceivable that an encounter with the police might be helpful at this stage. That's as far as I can go, Mr. West, unless you can be more specific. For instance, has the boy committed any offence?"

There was real anxiety in his voice, and that told its own story.

"I'm here because he made a statement which might later be used in evidence in an important case, and I want to try to be sure that he's trustworthy. Would you think it possible that he could be influenced to make a statement which wasn't true?"

"Between these four walls – yes, he could."

"Thank you," said Roger, and leaned back on an uncomfortable hardwood chair. "Is he in school now?"

"Yes. But I'm not sure that if you interview him here he would co-operate."

"I'd rather be sure he's here while I go and interview his mother," Roger said.

The headmaster's expression changed.

"Oh, that's good. He'll be here all day; he lives too far away to go home for lunch!" The headmaster stood up as Roger did, and rounded the desk with a hand outstretched. "I hope you won't think I've been unhelpful, and I hope you'll believe that the boy has quite remarkable abilities. I wish he – and in fact I wish all – boys would look you in the eye as squarely as yours. *Very* nice lads – and his headmaster has the highest opinion of Martin."

Roger smiled. "Nice of you to say so."

As he was ushered out by the headmaster in person, he heard a chorus of voices, raised in a song, clear and lovely on the bright morning air.

As the door of 101 Hadworth Palace Road opened, swing music came cavorting from behind the woman who stood with a hand on the door, looking West up and down. She was in her forties, had brassy hair, big bosom supported tightly from underneath and making the most of cleavage, and a pale-coloured flowered frock. From the radio or the record player behind her there came a roll of drums which must have been born in New Orleans, rising to a kind of triumphant crescendo.

"Good morning," Roger said.

Her eyes were bold yet shifty, and she didn't move away from the door.

"Is it about the insurance? Because if it is "

"I'd like a word with you about your son, Clive."

"*Oh*," said Mrs. Harrison, and moved back a little, as if all tension had gone. She couldn't find the money to pay her weekly insurance, which might be a pointer to her circumstances. "I suppose you're another school inspector. I don't know why you're always picking on my Clive, he's a good boy, and a lot more clever than most of them."

"I'm told he's very clever indeed." Roger smiled, and moved into the hallway.

"Well, you'd better come in."

She wasn't very gracious, but didn't want to be too stand-offish, Roger guessed. She was interested in him as a man, probably subconsciously she was already flaunting her body.

She was like Rose Jensen about the mouth, and had the same eyes, too—

Realisation of the possible truth came into Roger's mind like a bullet. She was so like Rose Jensen that they might almost have been sisters.

Were they?

Mrs. Harrison led the way into a small front room with a low ceiling. Unexpectedly, it was well-furnished and nicely kept, with the clean, polished look which told of a house-proud woman. Mrs. Harrison was clean and fresh, too, and lightly made up; more wholesome in some ways than the brassy hair and the rather loose mouth had suggested. She looked at him as if not sure whether to smile or not.

"Well, what has Clive been up to?"

He ought to tell her he was from the police, but if he did, she would almost certainly freeze up. If he didn't and she complained, that would be another piece of trouble for him; but nothing like as black as the trouble he was in. He judged her to be pretty shrewd, and not easy to fool for long.

"He said that he was in Page Street, Elwell, on Monday evening, Mrs. Harrison, and I've reason to believe that he wasn't. Why did he lie?"

Her colour ebbed. Fright touched her eyes, and she made a woman's automatic gesture, put a hand at her breast and for a moment held her breath. Roger had this much satisfaction before he saw the change in her expression, and the colour flow back to her cheeks. It was almost startling to see how the sparks leapt to her eyes.

"I'd like to know who you think you are, calling my Clive a liar! If he says he was in Page Street, then he was, and that's that and all about it."

"Supposing it can be proved that he was somewhere else?"

"Well, it can't be, because he was there. My Clive isn't a liar, and it will take more than a snooping policeman to make me change my mind about that. You think I don't know who you are, don't you? Why, I could tell your smooth face anywhere. My Clive's a truthful boy, and he was in Page Street on Monday night, *and* I can prove it."

Roger watched her.

Her silence was uneasy, after the outburst; she wasn't used to people who took what she handed out and didn't try to throw it back in her face. Her eyes, fine and grey, darted to and fro.

She might be able to prove what she said about Clive.

"And I haven't time to stand here wasting time with you or anyone else." Mrs. Harrison's voice was shrill. "I've got my housework to do."

"Why was Clive in Page Street?" Roger asked quietly. "Had he gone to see his aunt?"

Mrs. Harrison caught her breath.

She was no good at all at dissembling, and that was the most hopeful thing Roger discovered. Put her in the witness-box, and she would be like wax in a good counsel's hand. Here was a witness Samuelson's stooges ought to have; Samuelson should have been digging up this kind of thing, and not being smart.

Mrs. Harrison still hadn't answered, and her breathing was very quick and agitated.

Then, Roger realised what he should have noticed before: the music had quietened. It was still in the background, but the volume had been turned down; and he guessed that was because someone was listening to this conversation, probably close to the door.

"You—you've no right to stand there asking me questions. I don't have to answer!"

"All right, please yourself," Roger said brusquely, and pushed past her towards the door, going much more quickly than she had expected. He felt it yield. He opened the door, and a man standing close to it moved back hastily. He was a hardy, tight-lipped man whom Roger had never seen before, handsome in his fashion, with dark hair which grew far back on his forehead. He was in shirt sleeves, and wearing braces, as if he was one of the household.

"Good morning," Roger said curtly.

He swung round towards the street door, which was closed, opened it and strode into the street. By then the woman had joined the man in the passage, and they stared at Roger as he moved towards the left; his taxi was at a corner. They didn't come into the street, and he didn't spend any time looking round for them, but hurried towards the taxi. He felt quite sure that Mrs. Harrison simply hadn't known what to answer when he had let her know that he guessed she was the dead woman's sister. Mrs. Harrison would do whatever she was told, her son would probably do what he was told or paid to do, also – but the woman didn't know how to cope with unexpected situations.

Taxi driver Nobb was just sitting.

"Given up reading?" Roger asked as he climbed in.

"These papers!"

"You're telling me. Nearest telephone kiosk, please."

"Oke," Nobb said; "there's one on the corner." He drove only fifty yards and pulled up at a spot, where a telephone kiosk stood empty. Two policemen were standing on the opposite corner, and Roger glanced across, but did not think they recognised him. It was the oddest feeling, to be apprehensive of men on the Force.

He dialled Whitehall 1212, and when the operator answered, asked in a flat voice which couldn't be recognised as his own: "Chief Inspector West, please."

"He's not in, sir. Superintendent Cortland is handling his cases."

"I'll talk to Chief Inspector Sloan, please."

"Very good, sir."

So Jay had passed the case on to Cortland, a senior man, not to one of the men who might have special sympathy for another C.I. That wasn't surprising. He mustn't put Sloan on the spot, but here was a message he had to get over.

"Sloan speaking ..."

"Mr. Sloan, I've a message for you from Chief Inspector West," Roger said in the same fiat, impersonal tone; it wasn't likely that Sloan would recognise it. "He strongly recommends that the boy witness, Clive Harrison, be questioned, and that his mother and a man now at the house in Hadworth Palace Road be watched. He thinks it is extremely important."

Sloan said sharply: "Who's speaking?"

"I'm just passing on a message, sir, and—"

"If you see West, tell him he's wanted at the Yard at once," Sloan said, and there was no doubt about the intensity of his feeling.

"All right, I will," Roger promised.

Two minutes' talk with Sloan would yield nearly everything he needed to know, but it might be overheard on the Yard exchange, and if it were, could get Sloan into a lot of trouble. Roger rang off. Sloan would pass this message on to Cortland; Cortland was too sound a man to take chances, and would soon get after Clive Harrison and his mother. If it was once established that the boy was lying, it would open the new field of investigation right up.

"Where to now?" asked the cabby.

"Henrietta Street, Covent Garden," Roger replied. "This end of it. Make it as fast as you can, will you?"

As Roger sat back and the taxi started off, Bill Sloan opened the door of Superintendent Cortland's office, and saw the big man, in his shirt sleeves and with his hair rumpled and untidy, sitting squarely behind his desk and pulling at a pipe badly burned at one side. At sight of Sloan, he pushed some papers away and asked shrewdly in his deep voice: "Sure it wasn't West himself?"

"It didn't sound like him," Sloan said.

"Shouldn't think he could fool you," said Cortland, and looked searchingly into Sloan's clear eyes. Cortland's eyes, rather dark brown in colour, were opaque-looking and cloudy. His face had an unhealthy, sallow look, his big hands were almost ugly. "Sloan, take a tip from me, will you? Don't go playing West's game. I don't know what he's up to, but he's a damned good copper and probably isn't wasting his time, but he could be getting himself in really bad with the Assistant Commissioner. You're known as one of West's oldest cronies, so don't you go and put a foot wrong. Apart from anything else, it would be the last thing West'd want."

"Thanks," said Sloan. "I won't forget. But isn't there any way to make Jay realise that Handsome's often worth two or three of us?"

"No, there isn't a way, even if it's true," Cortland said. "Now, exactly what was this message?"

Sloan told him.

"Done anything?"

"I thought I'd better check with you, first."

Cortland hesitated.

As the senior superintendent, he had to be on Jay's side. As a man with a reputation for being interested only in his job and in himself and his advancement, he was behaving much better than Sloan had expected, but there would be limits to his helpfulness. He sat scowling, as if at a prospect he disliked, and Sloan sensed a kind of struggle going on in his mind.

Then he said abruptly: "Okay. Have two men watch this Mrs. Harrison. All the usual routine; must be some reason for West wanting it done. Have someone outside the school and check young Harrison, too. If West thinks he's lying, it might mean the case against Quist could show some nasty gaps, and we'd better know sooner than later, even if it isn't what *he* wants. Get it all done quick, Sloan. Jay's in another of these damned conferences with the other A.C.s. I want this job in hand before he comes out."

Sloan was already at the door.

"Right!"

He'd do this job well.

Cortland worked alone in his office for the next half-hour. Usually a C.I. was with him, but this man's desk was empty this morning; he was on sick leave. Every now and again Cortland answered the telephone, and at half-past twelve he lifted the receiver again, to hear Miss Foster's prim and precise voice.

"The Colonel would like to see you at once, Mr. Cortland, please."

"Coming," Cortland said.

He stood up, looking heavy and shaggy, suddenly took a small comb from his hip pocket and ran it through his hair, then shrugged himself into his coat, and made sure that his tie was fairly straight. His reputation at the Yard was one of unimaginative soundness, built on a deep, exhaustive knowledge of routine in all its branches. He walked slowly along the passages until he reached Jay's outer office, and went in without tapping. That was his unspoken disregard for Miss Foster; there was marked antipathy between them.

"He in?"

"He would like you to go straight in, please," the girl said, and flicked a little handle on an office communication machine. "Superintendent Cortland is here, sir."

"Right," a voice sounded.

Cortland opened the door of the other office after a heavy tap. He closed it behind him while the Colonel signed some papers on his desk. The Colonel pushed these aside, and then sat erect and unmoving, clean-shaven, long-jawed, looking as if he was about to go on parade.

"Sit down, Cortland."

"Thanks." Cortland chose a wooden armchair.

"Has anything of particular importance come in while I've been with the Commissioner?"

"Found an old woman over at Ligate, strangled. Division's asked for *Fingerprints*. I sent Morgan over," Cortland said. "Otherwise, nothing much."

"Is there any information about West?"

"Not direct from West, sir," Cortland said, and passed on the message in his deep voice. "He's still on the job, anyhow; when he sticks he's like glue."

"I see. What have you done?"

"Having the boy and the woman watched. I wasn't sure how long you'd be upstairs."

The Colonel appeared to consider this for several seconds, and then he said: "Give me your blunt opinion, Cortland. Is West deliberately staying away from here, or is he following his usual custom – of working entirely on his own in the hope of getting quick and sensational results?"

Cortland took his time answering, and the expression in the Colonel's eyes suggested that he had prejudged the issue. Then Cortland said with great deliberation: "I should say he's keeping away. I should say he's got a line that he thinks ought to be followed, and he wants to see it through himself. He probably thinks that if he reports here in person or comes in, you'll suspend him pending an inquiry into what happened last night, and he'd rather get this job finished before he has to be stood off. That's my reading of it. Don't think it's far wrong either."

The Colonel looked almost smug.

"How long has he gone on thinking that he is the only man capable of carrying out specific investigations, Cortland?"

Cortland took his time again, and then rumbled: "When I first dealt with West – must be ten years ago – I thought he was the cockiest young swine on the Force. Brilliant, but cocky. Couldn't stand him at any price. He couldn't stand me much, either. Since you've asked, I might as well tell you to your face, sir, I don't like West. Not as a person, I mean – we've rubbed each other up the wrong way too often. But we get along now. If I've got a sticky case, I'd rather have West on it than anyone else. He might be a bit high-handed with – with me, f'r instance – but I don't think it's intentional, and on routine he doesn't often put a foot wrong. It's easy to forget—" Cortland had been speaking more and more slowly, and now his voice trailed off, as if he wasn't quite sure how to finish.

Jay wasn't helping him; Jay sat as if disapprovingly, looking straight into his eyes.

"What is it easy to forget, Cortland?"

"Best men we've got are all individualists," Cortland said. "No use keeping 'em on too tight a rein."

"Their influence on the general discipline doesn't alarm you?"

Cortland hesitated, and then waved his big hands.

"Never given it much thought."

"Ah," said the Colonel, as if that was exactly the answer he had expected. "I appreciate your frankness and your loyalty to the men under your command. Now"—he was quite brisk—"I want West here, and I want him quickly. I shall give him an opportunity of explaining what happened at his home last night, but in view of the effect of the incident on public opinion, whatever his explanation, I shall suspend him. I'm sure you realise that is inevitable. However, I am reluctant at this stage to do anything which might attract undue attention – from the newspapers, for instance. I propose to ask all Divisions to watch for West, and to request – instruct – him to report here at once. I hope he isn't likely to refuse to obey a specific instruction."

"He isn't beyond doing even that."

"I see," said the Assistant Commissioner, with acid disapproval. "See that the message gets to the Divisions and of course the Information Room, will you? I will confine this to our metropolitan and the City area; we won't go to the Home Counties forces yet. Have West report to you, and advise me as soon as he's here."

"Right-ho," said Cortland, and heaved himself to his feet.

The message reached all the London Divisions and the City of London police a little after half-past one. By two o'clock there wasn't a policeman in London not keeping his eyes open for Chief Inspector West. By two o'clock practically every senior policeman knew exactly what this meant; they had already heard rumours of the trouble between West and the new Assistant Commissioner.

At five-past two Sloan lifted his telephone and asked for Cortland, and the moment he was answered, he said: "That Clive Harrison kid left school, just before our man got there this lunch-time, and didn't turn up again after lunch. He didn't go home, as far as I can find out. What'll we do?"

Chapter Fourteen

Out?

Pegg's warehouse in Henrietta Street was cheek-by-jowl with Covent Garden market. An all-pervasive smell of fruit, vegetables and flowers was strong in Roger's nostrils as he stepped out of the taxi and studied the front of the premises. In fact, this was a shop, with *T. Pegg* written in black on green on the fascia board, which needed repainting. *Every Kind of Box and Packing Material,* the legend ran. There was an open door at one side, and shutters were down in front of the shop itself, suggesting that Theophilus Pegg's business opened more or less at the same hours as the market, which was half closed by now.

The staircase was narrow.

At the top was a small landing and a door marked: *Inquiries.* Roger thought he heard a girl say: "Yes, Mr. Pegg?"

He tried the door marked *Private*; it was locked. So he had no choice but to try *Inquiries.* A girl was coming out of another room, and she closed the door behind her with a snap. The way she looked at Roger suggested that she knew he had been coming and was wary of him; perhaps he had been spotted from a window above the shop. This girl might have been in any office anywhere in London; youngish, prettyish, neatly dressed, with fair hair which was a little untidy at the ends.

"Good afternoon."

"I'd like to speak to Mr. Pegg, please."

"I'm sorry, Mr. Pegg is out."

Roger looked her up and down. The response came too quickly and glibly, and he was almost sure that she had just spoken to Pegg; but girls were used to lying about their bosses being in, and she didn't turn a hair.

"Do you know when he will be back?" Roger turned on all his charm in a smile.

"He didn't say."

"Is he likely to be back this afternoon?"

"Well, he might and he might not."

It would be easy to lift up the flap in the counter and open the door through which she had just come; but there was the girl as witness, and Roger had no right to force his way in anywhere – and no time to wait too long to see Pegg.

"I'm sorry to be so insistent," Roger said, "but it is extremely important. Can you ask someone else if they can tell me when he'll be back?"

The girl hesitated, and then turned away quickly, muttered: "I'll try," and went into the other room. The door closed behind her firmly. Roger opened the flap, stepped through, and kept his ear close to the door, but it was more solid than it looked, and almost sound-proof. He could just hear a mutter of voices. He glanced round at piles of small boxes and cartons, and saw many of them addressed on Saxby's labels to various cities in Africa. There were stacks of a red label saying: *"Saxby's Air Freight Service."*

There were other stationery compartments, holding letter-headings, envelopes and oddments, some in black print, some in red; and there were several different designs of printing. He pulled out a sheet of letter-heading, and read:

Cole & Co.
Modern Fuel for Modern Fires

He felt a quickening of excitement as he looked at others, and then opened some letters and thumbed through them quickly, to check his first discovery.

Pegg had something to do with all the small businesses whose cheques Quist said had been altered, although his name didn't appear on any. Quist's memory hadn't played him false.

Roger closed the books and put them away as he heard someone else coming up the stairs. He moved quickly to the other side of the counter.

The newcomer didn't come in, but went to the other, locked door. Roger moved again, opened this door a crack, and was in time to see a man stepping into the other room. As he went, the man turned sideways to Roger, without knowing that he was being watched.

It was the man who had been at Mrs. Harrison's.

"Now I'm quite sure," Roger thought, with a curious kind of reluctant elation. "If there's collusion between the witnesses, the case against Quist can be broken wide open. He got on to something all right."

He closed the door.

The girl came out.

"I'm sorry," she said, "but no one knows whether Mr. Pegg will be back today; he's not expected until sometime tomorrow."

"I see; thanks," Roger said. "May I leave a message?"

"Oh, sure."

"Tell him that Chief Inspector West of Scotland Yard will call on him at ten o'clock tomorrow morning."

"All right," she said.

She wasn't surprised by his name and rank, which meant she had been warned; almost certainly Pegg had seen him come in. Now Roger went out. He listened at the door marked *Private,* and could just hear a mutter of voices, that was all. The door was locked again. He went quickly down the stairs, making plenty of noise, but hesitated at the front, because he caught a glimpse of a uniformed police sergeant standing at a corner and talking to two market porters. As he waited, he faced up to several things. It wouldn't be long before he would be compelled to report to the Yard, and it might be wise to go now that he had reasonable evidence of collusion. He doubted if it was strong enough yet, though; and before he did anything else, he wanted to eat; he was famished.

He wanted time to think, too. As far as he could judge, five people were concerned in the collusion.

He made a mental note of them.

Mrs. Kimmeridge.
Clive Harrison.
Mrs. Harrison.
Theophilus Pegg.
The man from Mrs. Harrison, who was now upstairs.

"Once we work on Mrs. Harrison, she'll start to crack," he told himself.

The police sergeant cycled off. Roger went out, feeling uneasily that it would be impossible to play this hide-and-seek business much longer. He couldn't see Pegg without spending a lot of time here, but might have a chance to see Mrs. Kimmeridge again – the first possibly false witness. He stepped into the taxi, aware of a rather long, testing stare from Nobb. Was he beginning to suspect that something was wrong? In a flash of time Roger was filled with depression. He was only on the fringe of this affair; he believed that five people at least were lying, five people were prepared to see an innocent man condemned; but it was only guesswork. It didn't even amount to a theory he would have taken to Chatworth had Chatworth been in his sunniest mood.

Chatworth, Cortland, Colonel Jay – these and any of his superiors would want to know a lot more before they attempted to take any action.

Why should so many people lie?

Why should they gang up on Michael Quist?

Had Quist's arrival at Page Street at that particular time been really coincidental? Could Henry and his daughter have conspired to send him there?

Was he, Roger, justified in wanting to believe Quist, and assuming therefore that all the others were liars? He knew that it was more than assuming; he had seen the effect on Mrs. Harrison and on Charles Henry when they had been challenged, but that was all he had – and impressions weren't evidence. Impressions could get him off to a good start, that was all.

They hadn't started to move.

He hadn't told Nobb where to go.

"Staying here all night?" Nobb asked. "Or are you going home to dinner?"

Roger found a grin.

"You hungry, too?"

"Famished. I was on duty at seven this morning."

"We'll have a quick lunch at a market café," Roger said. "You probably know the best one."

"Okay, I'll take you there." Nobb let in his clutch and started off. Roger leaned back – and then, almost as an afterthought, looked out of the small rear window. He saw a man on a motor-cycle start off from the kerb outside the little warehouse, and he hadn't been there when Roger had come away. He didn't recognise the man, a youngster, who wore goggles and a crash helmet; not only good for safety, but good for concealment. The motor-cycle came on, close behind. It wasn't surprising that it stayed behind for some time, for they crawled behind a huge lorry laden with boxes marked: *Produce of South Africa*. When they turned a corner and stopped outside a small café, with a board outside saying: *3 Course Meal, 3/-* the motor-cycle passed.

It would be wise to keep his eyes open for it.

The café was hot and steamy, few people were in it. A tired-looking woman came up almost as soon as he and Nobb had sat down, with a steaming bowl of soup. The taxi-driver decided that this was the time to study racing form, and took a folded newspaper out of his pocket; he ate noisily as he read. Outside there was a rumble of heavy market traffic, that was all.

But the motor-cyclist kept the café in sight.

A little while earlier, Theophilus Pegg put down the telephone in his office overlooking Henrietta Street, and pinched his plump jowl while scowling at the window. Then he edged his chair a little nearer the window, so that he could see into the street. He saw the taxi draw up, saw West get out, and immediately telephoned the receptionist.

"There's a man named West coming up, a policeman in plain clothes. Just tell him I'm not in. Don't let him guess I'm here."

He heard West arrive, sat there on edge for a while, and then heard a tap at the locked door which was at the head of the stairs. He opened this cautiously, and stepped outside as the man there started to come in.

"Careful, Syd; he's in the other office."

The door closed.

The man named Syd, from Mrs. Harrison's house, was now wearing a dark blue jacket and a collar and tie. His short hair was smarmed back from his forehead, his bright, very dark eyes had a look of quick intelligence. He turned the key in the lock, and then went across to the other door, and listened.

They heard West go downstairs.

"Chick ready?" Syd asked.

"Should be round the corner by now; I told him to not make it too obvious," Pegg said. "He'll be on his motorbike; he's reliable."

"He'd better be," Syd said. He sat on an upright chair, the wrong way round, so that he could lean on the back. He was chewing with slow, slight rhythmic movements, which hadn't been noticeable at first, and kept showing his strong, white teeth. "West's been to the school, been to Kate's – saw him there myself – been to Henry's, been here. He's caught on."

"He's caught on all right," Pegg said, and stopped at that. "What did he say to Kate?"

"Said he knew the kid had been lying."

"Who started him on this track? How—"

"I don't know, and I don't see that it makes any difference," Syd said. "What I want to know is, why did you fix to frame Quist? It was crazy."

"You seemed to think it was smart at the time," Pegg said nastily. "You put the kid up to his piece too; that wasn't exactly a stroke of genius. It was okay while no one knew anything, but now the cops will bust it wide open. I told some of 'em that Henry was at the Rose and Crown a couple of hours from eight-thirty on Monday night, but someone else in the pub might have noticed he stepped out for twenty minutes. Once this job begins to crack—"

"Listen, Theo," Syd said softly; "you're the brains behind this outfit; I don't pretend to be. And you said we had to fix Quist. When I telephoned and told you Quist was in the pub and was going after Henry, you said okay, put Rose away, it was a perfect set-up to frame Quist. So I put her away. Is that right or isn't it?"

Pegg said quietly. "It looked good, Syd."

"It looked good to me, but you're the one who always thinks twice, and sees all the snags. Why didn't you this time?"

"When I saw I'd gone wrong I tried to have Quist put away, didn't I? I can have an off day," Pegg went on, and his eyes looked angry. "We going to fight between ourselves, or are we going to keep ourselves out of trouble?"

"Tell me how," Syd said gruffly.

"We've just got to stall for a day or so," Pegg said. "We can get clear if we do. All we need is a bit more time."

Syd's eyes were narrow as he tipped the chair forward and seemed intent on putting all his weight on one leg.

"Maybe, West's good, but what I don't understand is, he's doing it all on his own."

"West is?"

"Yep."

"Got a reputation for that, ain't he?"

"Maybe," Syd said, "but I don't understand it. Going round by taxi, too."

"That could be to fool us."

"Could be," Syd admitted, and scowled. "Haven't heard that anyone's been with him at all, but there's a dick outside Clive's school. I had to get the kid away quick. If the Yard had had a real go at him before we told him what to say, he might've cracked. He'll be okay now; I've talked to him."

"Where is he?"

"Chick's place."

"I'm not sure that was wise," Pegg said.

"Don't start blaming me if things go wrong," Syd said, and his mood was still ugly; his resentment rose quickly to the surface. "I had to make sure that kid knew what to say. What's surprising if he goes off for a day? He often plays truant, and everyone knows it."

Pegg didn't answer.

"Copper outside Kate's place, too," Syd went on. "She nearly fell through the floor when West talked to her; it was a good thing I was there. But she won't make any mistake in future; I told her that if she did she'd end up the way her sister ended up. She'll keep her trap shut, and there's no reason why West or anyone else should go for her. They'll go for the kid."

Pegg said: "We'd better make sure that none of our crowd goes to see Kate, or Lucy over at Page Street. Henry's fixing that cash – he's got to fix the books first, but he'll have it done by tonight. When we've got the cash we'll put him away, and then who'll be able to talk about us? Quist won't be any danger then. No one will, Syd. We always knew it would be over quick, and we've made a nice picking. Today West's on our tails, but in a day or two we'll be clear of him. Everything's laid on."

Syd's eyes had not lost their glitter.

"The main thing is, *are* we okay?"

"Henry's our weak link, but we can trust him to keep quiet now his neck's at stake," Pegg insisted. "You say you've fixed Kate, and we know Lucy'll keep as tight as a drum."

The telephone rang. He lifted the receiver, said: "Pegg," and listened. "Okay, watch him," he said abruptly, and rang off. He was frowning when he looked at Syd.

"That's Chick," he announced. "West's having a meal at Gordie's Café, with that cabby." He waved as if at some unimportant interruption. "The main job's okay, then. We just stick to our stories. The cops can break their necks trying, but they can't prove anyone's lying until we've got everything sewn up."

Syd's jaws still worked on the gum.

"I don't understand about West," he said stubbornly. "What else has he got? What's he on his own for? Why'd he go round the corner to a market café for a meal? That's what I want to know. Think there's any way we can get at West?"

Pegg didn't answer.

"Don't give me that one about cops being incorruptible," Syd went on. "They'll sit up and beg if the price is high enough."

Pegg was rubbing his hands together, as if nervously.

"We could certainly use some more time; if we could keep West away for a couple of days it would be fine."

"Who would you work through?"

"Kate," answered Syd, very slowly and thoughtfully. "She'll say exactly what we tell her to, and nothing else. She could doll herself up a bit, and then send West a message saying she had something to say to him. That wouldn't surprise him. Or *we* could tell him she wants to see him."

"I don't know that I like—" Pegg began.

"Listen; we all have to do things we don't like, sometimes," Syd said. "I didn't like croaking Rosie, but we couldn't afford to let her live, and we can't afford to let the cops get any one of us, can we? West is on to Clive, so I've told the kid what to say if he's questioned again. If they ask him why he didn't say Rose was his aunt, he'll explain that when they questioned him first he thought that his Auntie Rose was in some kind of trouble and he didn't want to make it any worse. So if we can shake West off, we'll be on easy street."

"You mean, if we could get him to compromise himself with Kate. Is that it?"

"That's it. Remember what happened last night." Syd allowed himself a thin smile; he could never know how much he looked and behaved like Colonel Jay. "West's in some kind of trouble already. If we could get him in bed with Kate, and take a picture, that would be really something. You still got some of those knock-out drops we used on Dandy last year? Put him out for a couple of hours, remember?"

Pegg said: "I think I have, but—" He broke off.

"Getting worried, Theo?" Syd asked sneerily.

Pegg thumped his desk with the flat of his hand, in sudden anger.

"Of course I'm getting worried, worried as hell! I don't like being rushed, I don't like any of it. But I can't see any better way than trying to work on West through Katie. It wouldn't be the first time she's made a man forget what he went to see her about, and it can't make things any worse. How are we going to tell West she wants to see him?"

Syd sat chewing.

"I'm Kate's cousin, and he'll put two and two together," Pegg went on tensely. "So I can give him a message. Yes, that's it; I can give him a message. No reason why I shouldn't see my own cousin. Maybe I'll get something out of West about Clive, too." Pegg stood up, lifting the telephone as he did so, looking very worried and yet somehow compelling attention. "Betty, leave the switchboard for a minute. Go along the road and see if Chick's still at the end of the street. If he is, go into Gordie's Café and ask the man West if he'd come along and see me. Say I've just got back."

"Sure," the girl said.

Pegg put down the telephone, and began to chew the nail of a little finger.

It was a good meal.

Roger dabbed his lips with a paper serviette, and stood up. He had already paid the bill, and the taxi-driver had gone out ahead. He wondered if the motor-cyclist was still watching, and decided to stroll towards the corner and see for himself, but as he went out of the shop into the sunlight, the girl from Pegg's warehouse came hurrying along. She had very high heels, and wobbled a little on spindly legs. Without smiling, she stopped in front of him; this was the last development he had expected.

"Excuse me, Mr. West, Mr. Pegg is back, and he says would you be good enough to go and have a word with him? He'd be ever so grateful, really."

It wasn't only unexpected, it smelt to high heaven; but there was no point in hesitating, because he still wanted to see Pegg. So Roger flashed his most amiable smile, and obviously startled the girl.

"Yes, I'll be along in a few minutes."

"Oh, thanks ever so."

The girl hurried back, her step still mincing, the frill at the end of her skirt frisking about her legs just below the knee. Roger strolled towards the taxi. The motor-cyclist had gone; his appearance could have been a coincidence. The taxi-driver was leaning against his cab and listening to a porter telling some tale about his wife and a lodger in loud tones which brought smirks and grins from a dozen people nearby. A man wheeled a barrow, laden with bananas, almost over the cabby's toes.

"I'll be half an hour, Nobb," Roger said. "Will you wait?"

"Oke."

"Thanks."

"Be able to take a week's holiday after this," Nobb quipped. "At the public expense, you might say."

Roger grinned.

Then he saw two policemen, standing together not far away; if they looked up now they would almost certainly recognise him, and he felt his heart beating uncomfortably. He didn't want to avoid them deliberately; a trained constable had a habit of knowing when a man was doing that. So he stopped and looked into a fruit warehouse, then saw the pair go down a side street. He didn't like the evasion at all, but hurried towards Pegg's warehouse. On this side of it there was a small paved alley, a short cut to one of the market halls; several trolleys and barrows were being trundled along it. Roger saw them, but didn't see a man standing just behind a tall pile of crates. Even if he had, he would not have recognised the motor-cyclist without his goggles.

He reached the crates, and then heard Bill Sloan call softly: "Roger!"

He swung round, really startled, his heart pounding. Sloan hadn't moved. The crates gave him good cover from the street, but not from the entrance to the market hall.

Roger went to him.

"I don't know what you're planning to do," Sloan said. "So far as I'm concerned I haven't seen you, but every copper on the Force is looking out for you, and asking you to report to the A.C. The Yard's buzzing with it; the Divisions soon will be, too. You're taking a hell of a risk."

"It's taken," said Roger. "I wish you hadn't stuck your neck out, but I'm damned glad to see you." He kept his voice low. "How about the Harrisons, mother and son?"

"The boy's gone off somewhere; apparently he often plays truant," Sloan said. "We're having a man watch Mrs. Harrison. I passed your message on to Cortland; he reacted better than I thought he would."

"Corty's all right," Roger said. "Wish I knew where that boy's gone, but there's no case for putting a call out for him. Anything else in?"

"Not much. Did a pretty thorough job at the Hadworth Bank, and there's nothing to suggest that Henry's in money trouble. Saxby's say they'll get their accountants to check all bank figures, but it's a big job and will take days, and that will be too late for you. Had another go, through Brown, at Mrs. Henry and the daughter, Sybil, but they wouldn't come across any more. Samuelson was at the Yard for an hour this morning; there was a conference – him, Jay and the Commissioner. That's why I say you ought to show up."

"There are one or two things I ought to do before I come back," Roger said quietly. "Nothing would stop Jay from standing me off now, so I might as well make a job of it. Just in case anything goes really wrong, and I am taken off the case—"

He broke off.

Three men pushing wheelcarts trundled by them; a fourth came striding along with eight or nine round baskets on his head, quite unconcerned.

"Well?" Sloan asked, looking about as if he was equally anxious not to be seen.

"Collusion among the witnesses is the line to follow. Young Harrison is Rose Jensen's nephew, but tell Corty it's probably better to keep that to ourselves for a bit. All right?"

"Roger, why don't you stop this caper, and come back to the Yard?" Sloan demanded, and obviously he would have liked to take Roger back by force. His voice actually quivered in his earnestness. "You can pass all this on to Corty and me before seeing Jay. We'll follow it up, and while you're having a few days' rest—"

Roger broke in sharply.

"Sorry, Bill. I've been thinking about this all day. If Jay's decided to make an example, he'll make it good and proper. This could be my last case for a long time, could even be my last case. I'm going to try to see it through."

"I think you're a damned fool."

"Perhaps I think I'm a damned fool, too," Roger said. "If there's any urgent message, leave it with Janet, and I'll pick it up somehow or other."

"Pick it up is right," Sloan grumbled, and added gloomily: "Corty says he wouldn't be surprised if the next step is a call to pick *you* up. Jay's getting really mad."

"It's one of those things," Roger said.

Sloan eyed him searchingly, and then said with obvious reluctance: "I suppose it is. No use my trying any more, anyhow. I'll be seeing you."

Roger nodded, and turned away.

"I tell you I heard him say it," Chick the motor-cyclist breathed to Pegg and Syd. "I nipped into the jimmy, and heard every word. Actually said he wouldn't be surprised if the next stage wasn't to pick West up. West's in bad. There was something about having a rest, and the other copper said he ought to stop this caper."

He stopped, but still gasped for breath.

"You know what?" said Syd very softly. "West is out on a limb. All we've got to do is to push him off. Treat him gently, Theo; don't let him get away."

"I won't let him get away," said Pegg. "If we can fix West and all stick together, we'll be sitting pretty."

"It's a fine thing," Syd said sneeringly. "You get us in the trouble, I get us out. After this I'll be the master mind."

Pegg didn't speak.

Chapter Fifteen

New Angle

"You may very well say that it's none of my business," Samuelson said, in his most gentle voice, "but I can't help saying that I hope you won't let West get away with this, Mr. Assistant Commissioner. As we've just heard from Miss Henry, she did go to see him of her own accord. I'm glad to say that there was no effort on West's part to interfere with a witness who might be called for the defence. But for him to use such violence against members of the Press who were doing their public duty—" He broke off.

Colonel Jay looked exactly as he had when Cortland had talked to him earlier.

"I shall bear in mind what you say," he said. "Thank you for bringing this to my notice. And thank you for your information, Miss Henry." He looked at the girl, who was rising from her chair near a corner of his desk. "You have been very good."

She didn't speak.

She was dressed in a linen two-piece, and wearing a small hat of the same apple-green colour. She looked fresh and charming; if she felt worked-up she hadn't shown it since arriving here with Samuelson to see the Assistant Commissioner. Samuelson, with his benevolent expression, his silvery hair and pinkish complexion, might have been her father.

"You may be sure that if Mr. Quist is not guilty of the murder, we shall find out," Jay said. "I hope you will understand me when I say that if there should be any other item of information which you wish the police to know, it would be much wiser to come here and report, and not to go to the home of any individual."

"I think you forget how worried I was," Sybil said, quite firmly. "And I felt sure that I could get a hearing from Mr. West. There's one other thing I ought to say before we go."

"Yes, Miss Henry?"

"Mr. West didn't start the fighting last night; he was very strongly provoked. He didn't strike any one of the others before his son was attacked."

Samuelson shrugged, disparagingly.

Jay said: "Were you an eye-witness all the time, Miss Henry?"

"No, but—"

"How do you know who started the fracas?"

"I heard what was going on, and Martin West told me afterwards that —"

"A son would naturally side with his father," Samuelson put in smoothly, and Jay nodded. "I don't think we should take up any more of the Assistant Commissioner's time, Miss Henry. He asked you to come and tell him exactly what you saw happen, and I know he's grateful."

"Most grateful."

Sybil said, almost helplessly: "I don't seem to have helped. Colonel Jay—"

"My dear—"

"Yes. Miss Henry?"

"Would it be possible to see Mick—Mr. Quist—even for a few minutes?"

"I am afraid that is not possible," the Colonel said, and as the girl turned away, he went on in a voice which obviously had an edgier note in it: "Had you any knowledge of his association with Miss Jensen?"

Sybil caught her breath. "I don't believe he ever knew her."

"I'm sure we've stayed too long," murmured Samuelson. "Good day, Assistant Commissioner."

When they had gone, Jay stood looking out of the window, tight-lipped, watching a few people hurrying, many dawdling, the pleasure-boats on the river, and the stream of traffic flowing in either direction over Westminster Bridge.

Each year Roger interviewed hundreds, sometimes thousands, of different people. Each year his ability to judge their integrity and truthfulness became a little better. Each year his first-sight judgement was usually confirmed by results and events, but occasionally he was hopelessly wide of the mark. That made him wary of being emphatic in his opinion.

He had few reservations about Theophilus Pegg.

Pegg didn't do his job badly, though. He protested a little too much, was a little too earnest and virtuous, and too apologetic; and he had almost certainly been in the office when Roger had first called.

"... I do assure you, Mr. West, my cousin and I are very anxious indeed to help in every way we can; we wouldn't like any injustice done. As I've said, all we want is to see Miss Jensen avenged; no one ought to be allowed to get away with murder. I couldn't agree with you more about that. Ever since you called and told Kate – that's Mrs. Harrison, of course – that you were afraid that her son had lied, she's been very worried. Of course she sprang to his defence; what mother wouldn't? She wouldn't like to think he had told a falsehood which got other people into trouble. You know how boys are, Mr. West, and this boy isn't a *liar,* but like all of them at his age he does like the limelight, does like to attract attention to himself. I'm sure that if he did tell any falsehood, it was without malicious intent."

Roger said: "I hope you're right."

"Well, I'm sure I am," said Pegg. "I can't say that I know the boy didn't—er, exaggerate, shall we say?—but I'm positive it would be without malice. His mother thinks it might be very helpful if you would go and see her again, and she tells me – over the telephone, I haven't seen her, Mr. West – she tells me that she thinks she might have a little information about her sister's murder that might be helpful. You know that the two sisters saw very little of each other, don't you?"

"So little that Mrs. Harrison didn't come forward as a relation," Roger observed.

Nor had Pegg.

"I know, it was unfortunate," Pegg said smoothly; "but then she is a lady with an untarnished reputation, and you know how scandal affects one's so-called friends and neighbours. However, if you feel that she has nothing to say that might be helpful, I shall understand. She will be very disappointed, but—"

He broke off.

That there was a trick in this proposition stood out as plainly as Theophilus Pegg's addiction to whisky. That didn't mean that Roger shouldn't go and talk to the Harrison woman. He had scared them all, and they were going to try to cover up; it was essential to find out how, and he couldn't think of any other way. If things had been normal he would have waited, it wouldn't do Mrs. Harrison or Pegg any harm to sweat for a night; but he hadn't a chance of staying on the job beyond today.

So he had to hand it over now, or else agree to see the woman soon.

He had arranged for her house to be watched, and it wouldn't be easy to get in there without being seen by the Yard man. Probably it wouldn't even be possible, unless some kind of diversion was created; but he didn't intend to call on Pegg for help. Pegg was watching intently, and obviously his anxiety was real, not pretended. He was scared, Mrs. Harrison was scared, Henry was scared. It was a damned queer business. First Quist on a plate, now these people too, if he handled the job properly. Roger found himself thinking beyond that again, and wondering what lay behind it all. Why should five people gang up to save themselves, being so ruthless that they would gladly see an innocent man convicted? They couldn't be more vindictive towards Quist if they were setting out to frame him deliberately; if he had been an intended victim from the beginning.

Could they be ganging up on Quist because he *was* Quist, not simply because he had chanced to be in Page Street?

Had it been sheer chance?

Was Quist also lying, to save himself?

Roger hadn't wondered about that seriously before. He didn't want to concentrate on it now, but would have to. If he turned up at the Yard again with the case as confused as it was now, he could say goodbye to rank.

He'd probably have to do more than that, as he'd hinted to Sloan. It was in his mind, lurking as a horror in a nightmare. He might even have to say goodbye to the Yard.

Thoughts took so little time.

Pegg watched Roger, frowning and a little puzzled because he was taking so long to answer, but that was all. Pegg didn't know how many conflicting ideas had gone through Roger's mind, didn't know that Roger was coming rapidly to a decision: that he would have to try to get to the bottom of all of this alone if he was to stand any chance of getting out of trouble.

"Yes, I'll see Mrs. Harrison," he decided. "When will she be in?"

"Why, any time, Mr. West; you're very good to take the trouble. She's on the telephone, I'll give her a call." Pegg didn't overdo his satisfaction.

Roger said: "I can't tell you when I'll call, but I hope she'll be in when I do."

"Oh, she'll wait in; she's very anxious to put any misunderstanding right."

West stood up. "I hope she means it," he said. "Thanks, Mr. Pegg."

"It's a real pleasure to help the police at any time," Pegg said, and hurried ahead of him to open the door. "I really mean that, Mr. West, especially such a distinguished officer as you."

Roger kept a straight face …

The afternoon sun struck warm. He had been in the office for less than twenty minutes, but now the warmth seemed much greater and there were fewer people in the streets. Fruit and vegetable warehouses which had been opened, with vans being loaded outside, were closed. A few elderly men were sweeping up the rubbish, without any enthusiasm. The taxi was a little way along the road. Roger went towards it, watching, making sure that he wasn't followed.

He saw no trace of anyone.

It was nearly three o'clock. If he went straight to Hadworth Palace Road, it would suggest that he was much too anxious to see Mrs. Harrison. But how could he use the time? If he could call the Yard and give orders to Ibbetson and Brown, and work from there himself, he could fill every minute of the day, but now time threatened to hang heavily. The new angle on Quist was teasing him, too, and as he got into the taxi, he said: "We'll go to North Hadworth again – Laurel Avenue."

"What's the matter with the police cars today?" the cabby asked. "They gone on strike?"

"I don't want to let the people I call on know in advance who I am."

"That so?" Nobb turned round to look at Roger through the glass partition, and then said very quietly: "It's none of my business, Mr. West, but up at the shelter some of the chaps was saying that the sergeant on this beat asked them to give him the tip if they saw you. Said he's got an urgent message for you. You told me to keep my mouth shut, so I kept it shut."

Roger said warmly: "Thanks."

"Still want to go to North Hadworth?"

"Yes."

"As I said, it's none of my business," the taxi-driver said, and turned round.

He hadn't smiled.

It took them nearly half an hour to get through the early home-going traffic to North Hadworth, and to Laurel Avenue. Real warmth lay upon the suburb, and on the little houses with their neat gardens. Colourful garden umbrellas and swings showed here and there, deck-chairs were pulled up on the grass under the shade. Only the children played, but one gardening enthusiast pushed an old lawn-mower. There were two deck-chairs on the lawn at the side of Henry's house, but only one was occupied. As Roger got out of the taxi he couldn't be sure who it was; then he saw Sybil Henry look round, and start up from the chair at sight of him.

He hurried across, feeling the stinging heat of the sun. She looked so cool, in contrast. She seemed surprised and even anxious, too. *Could* she have conspired with her father to send Quist to Page Street?

"Mr. West, have you any news?"

"No news, just one or two more questions," Roger said apologetically. "I'm sorry to have to worry you again, but—"

"It's quite all right. Won't you sit down?"

"I mustn't stay," Roger said, and forced an easy-looking smile. "There aren't enough hours in the day! You told me that you felt quite sure that Mr. Quist did not know Miss Jensen."

"I still feel quite sure."

"Did you know any of Mr. Quist's friends?"

"Only—only some of the people at the tennis club."

"You didn't know any of his personal friends, or his family?"

She didn't answer at once, and Roger thought that she was preparing to freeze up.

"No," she said at last. "I did make it clear that we haven't known each other very long, didn't I?"

"Yes," Roger said. "It might help more if you knew him well. Miss Henry, has Mr. Quist ever suggested anything that might imply that he was worried, or in any kind of danger or difficulty?"

"None whatsoever."

"Has he ever given you any indication that he had a personal enemy, with cause for resentment—"

"Mr. West, why don't you believe the simple truth?" Sybil demanded, and her voice was pitched high. "Mr. Quist is quite well off, he has an excellent job and very good prospects. He has lived a perfectly normal life, and there is nothing sinister about him at all. Why don't you look for the real murderer?"

No: she hadn't conspired against Quist.

That was the moment when the garden gate opened, and Charles Henry came walking towards them.

Chapter Sixteen

Real Murderer?

Henry had probably heard the last words. Undoubtedly he had been within earshot. Now he stared at his daughter as he drew nearer, his face set and his eyes glittering; and his expression was a certain indication that he had heard. West saw him then as an old man; one to whom something had happened during the day to bring the years heavily upon him. His fists were clenched, and he strode with restrained vigour. As he drew close, Roger thought that he was going to strike his daughter.

He stood still, a yard away from her.

"Now I know what you've been trying to do," he said in a savage voice. "You've tried to damn your own father so as to save that swine Quist. You damned, heartless little ingrate, you're no daughter of mine." He thrust his face closer to hers; all the muscles and nerves were twitching. "Get out of my house, and don't come back. Pack all your belongings, and don't ever let me set eyes on you again. Why, I could choke the life out of Quist, after what he's done to me. And you've let him use you—"

His hands, crooked like claws, came up.

"Someone choked the life out of Rose Jensen," Roger said coldly, and stared at those big hands.

Henry darted a glance at them, too. He seemed to sway. He dropped his arms by his side, and swung towards the house, and Sybil turned as if to follow him.

"I shouldn't," Roger said. "Not yet."

As he spoke, Henry reached the side door of the house, and swung on his heel. Behind him was a background of bright green leaves and the gaiety of flowers, softness and beauty. But his mouth worked and he showed how ugly man could be.

"I didn't kill that woman, I didn't even know her, but Quist did. I can prove it, too. Don't you forget, West, I can prove it; you're not going to get away with this. Coming creeping round the place, turning my own daughter against me; you're a disgrace to the police. If you had any sense at all you'd know that Quist was lying about me. He didn't tell you the truth. But my own daughter would rather believe a scoundrel with a smooth tongue than—"

He broke off, choking on the words.

"If you can prove anything against Quist or anyone else, prove it now," Roger said.

Henry didn't speak, but turned away.

His wife appeared in the doorway, despairing.

Quite without warning, Henry seemed to double up. He fell into her arms, massive against her smallness, and began to cry.

There were tears in Sybil's eyes.

"Is there anything else you can tell me?" Roger asked gently.

"I've told you everything I can," she said, in a voice which threatened to break at any moment. "God knows I don't want to do anything to hurt my father, but I had to tell the truth." She lowered her voice, and repeated in a whisper: "I had to tell the truth."

Then she walked towards her mother and father.

Roger got into the taxi, carrying a vivid mental picture of Charles Henry hurling that pathetic defiance at him. If anything was certain, it was the burden on Henry's mind. Subjected to the right pressures at that moment, he would probably have broken down and told the truth, might even have confessed to the murder of Rose Jensen.

But was he the murderer? Was he right about Quist? Did his talk of 'proving it' mean anything? It had sounded like hopeless bluster;

for if Henry knew anything against Quist, why didn't he say what it was?

The taxi was still waiting.

"Going anywhere this time?" the cabby asked again.

"Sorry. First a telephone kiosk, then Hadworth Palace Road again, and stop right outside Number 101, will you?" Roger took five pounds from his pocket; two pounds more than the meter showed. "I'll pay you now. Wait for twenty minutes, and if I'm not out by then you carry on and I'll make my own way back to the Yard."

The cabby grunted.

It might be imagination, but he seemed to have developed a marked lack of enthusiasm since he had heard about the message from the Yard. He was puzzled, of course, and might have heard more than he had said. By now, rumour would have swollen to great scandal at the Yard and in the Divisions, and there would be the careless talkers even among the police. In a way it would be a relief to get to the Yard and see Jay; at least the tension would be relaxed, and Jay would have to study any report.

Roger dialled the Yard from the nearest kiosk, and asked for Sloan again. When Sloan answered, Roger used the assumed voice, and said: "Mr. West thinks it would be useful if the man at the front of 101 Hadworth Palace Road was off for half an hour, soon."

"What the devil—" Sloan began.

"Fix it, will you?" Roger urged in his normal voice, and rang off and went back to the cab.

They were approaching the station at Hadworth when a police car passed, and Roger saw it slow down, and then swing round. That might be routine, or it might be because the driver or passenger had seen and recognised him. He didn't turn round to look, but soon saw the car pulling alongside. The passenger peered towards him as if to make sure who it was. Once he saw him, he waved, then called out so that Roger could hear.

"Pull into the kerb, Nobb."

The taxi-driver, already slowing down, obeyed immediately. The police car pulled up in front, and both driver and passenger jumped out. That's what they would do if they were going to hold a man.

But their expressions did not suggest anything sensational, and they looked in at the same window, from the kerb.

"Good afternoon, Mr. West."

"Hallo. Trouble?"

"We've been looking for you most of the day, sir; there's an urgent request for you to communicate with Superintendent Cortland. Like to use our radio?"

"Good idea," said Roger. "Thanks." He got out, and walked with them. One man leaned inside and flicked on the radio, then they both stood by the car, showing no particular interest in what was being said.

There were the familiar noises; the Information Room; eagerness in the voice of the man who responded; and then, very heavy and deliberate, Cortland's voice.

"That you, West?"

"I hear you want to talk to me."

"That's right. Report here just as soon as you can, and make it snappy."

"Right," said Roger. "I've one other call to make before—"

"I shouldn't make it."

"Listen, Corty; I've been chasing this job all day. I've one more call to make, and then I think I'll have quite a story for you. If I don't make it now, I'll be throwing a day's work away. I'll come straight on to the Yard when I've finished here."

He didn't give the Superintendent a chance to argue, but switched off. He was sweating, because Cortland's tone had confirmed everything that Sloan had said, but he didn't see what else he could possibly have done.

"Okay, sir?" the patrolmen were bluff.

"Fine, thanks."

"Right, sir!"

They went back to their car, and Roger got into the taxi. He wondered if they would follow; instead, they turned the car and went on the way they had been going, and that gave some relief: at least there was no general call except for him to report.

The taxi-driver seemed more affable.

"Everything all right, sir?"

"Everything's always been all right." Roger got in and sat back, lit a cigarette, and brushed his hand over his forehead. He was sweating so much that he could shake the moisture from his hand. This was it: see Mrs. Harrison, and die! Crazy thought. Worm the truth out of her somehow, so that he could have a real story for the Yard, something he could back with proof. Because he hadn't any proof yet, only a succession of hunches and impressions supported by the discovery that Kate Harrison was Rose Jensen's sister, and Kate hadn't come forward voluntarily.

He saw no Yard man opposite Number 101; Sloan was a friend indeed. He went to the house. The taxi-driver waited until the door opened and Kate Harrison stood in front of Roger. Nobb waited until Roger had gone inside, waited twenty minutes and then moved off.

The sight of Kate Harrison shouted a warning.

Roger had realised that morning that she could be quite a woman. Then she had been about her housework, without make-up, and wearing that old, sloppy dress. Now she was made up to kill, and a man wouldn't be human who didn't feel something of her attention. She didn't overdo the neckline, or even the bra support; she didn't need to. She wore a short-sleeved dress of biscuit colour, with an edging of scarlet at the square neck, the sleeves and the hem; and it had huge scarlet buttons. Her hair was still brassy, but it looked as if she had been to the hairdresser since seeing him; it was soft, and it had quite a sheen. She'd put on a little mascara, but not too much; she was made up rather more than Janet would be, but no more than a lot of women. She had quite a smile, and was using it.

Roger couldn't mistake her intention; she was going to try to win him round. There was the light pressure of her cool fingers on his hot hand as she drew him into the room. He could be amused by it, but not so much as he would have liked; he was too worried, too sharply conscious of the fact that he had to get some evidence which would stand up to the closest scrutiny,

"It's ever so good of you to come," she said. "When my cousin Theo told me he'd caught you, I was ever so relieved – I shouldn't like to give you a wrong impression." Still with her cool fingers on his, she led the way into the front room. It was all so obvious, yet not really overdone.

She flashed a smile.

The blinds were half drawn, to shut out the bright sunlight which now struck the windows. The small but well-furnished room, with its pleasant *décor* and its good furniture, had a real charm. A table, standing knee high between two easy-chairs, was laden with melt-in-the-mouth-looking sandwiches and small cakes which looked delicious. There was half a rich fruit cake on a silver stand, and near it a silver teapot, a tray and a spirit lamp. Kate lit the lamp, and as the gentle flame swayed beneath the kettle, motioned to a chair, and said: "The water is nearly boiling, we'll soon have a cup of tea."

Mrs. Kimmeridge's opening gambit, too.

"Why don't you just sit back for a minute; you look so hot?" Kate suggested. "It's ever such a sticky day to go chasing around, isn't it? I *say*, would you like a wash while the kettle's boiling? You'll be ever so welcome."

It would be welcome, too.

Roger said: "That's a good idea, thanks," and tried to infuse some heartiness into his voice. He hadn't sat down. He felt so sure that this was the parlour and he was the fly, but that was all: she wanted to make a good impression, meant to try to ease the pressure off. This was the way she was out to fool him, by putting up a nice act of sweet innocence. But here was Circe; and here was the sister of a murdered woman whose son had given a false statement to the police, and who had disappeared before the police could question him again.

"I'll show you the way," said Kate, and they reached the door together; she made it a tight squeeze, then went ahead.

The curve of her hips from her small waist was quite something to see; so was the shape of her legs and the smallness of her ankles, near his eyes as she led the way up the narrow stairs.

The bathroom was small and bright, with cream tiles. "I'll just get you a clean towel," Kate said. "That one over there is Syd's—Mr. Sydney's, I mean; he's a lodger here, but he's almost one of the family. Now you've got everything you want, and when you come down there'll be a nice cup of tea waiting."

She went out.

Roger put his head on one side, looked at his reflection in the mirror, saw that he looked sweaty and sticky; there was even a streak or two of dirt at the side of his nose. Some picture! But a cold wash would do him a world of good.

As Kate reached the foot of the stairs, Syd appeared at the kitchen door. They stared at each other for a moment, and then Kate whispered: "Am I doing all right?"

"You're doing fine," Syd approved. "Don't forget to put the right sugar in his tea, and if he doesn't take sugar, make sure he has some of that jam."

"All right, Syd, but I don't understand—"

"You don't have to understand," Syd said, in a whispering voice. He glanced upwards, and could hear Roger moving about. "You tell him what I told you to, about Clive. Then tell him about knowing Quist was putting the wind up Rose. Get him guessing, see? He'll know there's a catch in it, but he won't know what catch. You just keep him there for half an hour after he's had the dope, then you go upstairs and get the boudoir ready. Better put on your best nighty; you're going to have your photo taken."

"I hope it's all right," Kate said uneasily.

Syd dropped a hand to her wrist, and gripped tightly. "It'll be all right if you do it the way I tell you to. We've got a cop on the run, and we're going to make sure he gets in worse. But don't you give anything away; you just act simple." He dropped her hand, and sneered: "Just be yourself!"

The bathroom door opened …

"Sugar?" asked Kate sweetly.
"Thanks."

"One spoonful or two?"

"One and a bit will be fine, thanks," Roger said, and ate another of the sandwiches; he hadn't tasted ham sandwiches like this for a long time. He kept telling himself that he would soon have to quicken the tempo, and stop this fencing; but he could use half an hour's relaxation, he was enjoying the tea, and this was one occasion when he relished the way a woman tried to twist him round her little finger.

He'd heard her explanation of Clive's reason for not saying that Rose Jensen was his aunt.

He'd heard her protest again and again that she hadn't realised that the murdered woman was her own sister, at first, because she didn't read the papers until the afternoon. She had intended to tell the police immediately, but it was such a shock and she hadn't known what to do for the best, then she'd developed such an awful headache.

He'd seen the way she watched him with those bright and attractive eyes, and knew that she was on edge, but there was no reason at all to believe that it was anything but nervous anxiety to impress him. It wasn't going to surprise him if she soon started the seduction gambit. Every now and again she leaned forward to hand him his cup, or sandwiches – which he could reach without trouble – or cake. Each time the square neck of her dress fell forward, each time it was impossible not to let his eyes drop, impossible not to see those soft, inviting curves.

The thing that worried him was a drowsy feeling.

He blamed reaction, He also tried to blame the fact that he had been on the go so much, but that didn't convince him; he had often been on the move quite as much, and doing his own driving in the bargain.

He blamed the heat.

He sat up determinedly about half an hour after he had come downstairs; this was the time to start asking questions, the time to try to break her down. It could easily be done, she was nervous enough already. He just wanted to get the right angle, judge the moment well, and start.

He couldn't get his mind to work properly.

He was so damned tired.

It was an impossible situation, he must jerk himself out of it.

"Mrs. Harrison—"

His speech was slurred, and he hadn't realised that before. It was the moment of understanding and of awful shock. He saw her leaning towards him. She had nothing in her hands now. She just leaned forward, as if commandingly. There she was, inviting him; there she was, a beauty in her way, smiling a triumphant smile. He tried to get up, but could not, for his head was swimming and his legs were weak. He had fallen for the oldest trick of all.

She was hugging him.

There was a man in the doorway, with a box.

A camera!

Chapter Seventeen

Missing

"What time do you say he spoke to you?" Colonel Jay asked, in that aloof, correct voice.

"A little after four o'clock," Cortland told him.

"And he promised to come after this one call?"

"Yes."

"Where was he?"

"Hadworth Station."

"And it is now half-past six," said Jay, glancing at his wrist-watch. "Did he suggest that the call he had to make would take very long?"

"Said it wouldn't."

"In other words, we now have a situation in which an officer of the department refuses to obey specific instructions from his commanding officer," said Jay, and the tone of his voice was freezing. "No word has come in, apart from that?"

"No."

"Cortland, we don't want to cause a scandal," said Jay decisively. "On the other hand, we must bring West here. It is outrageous that he should stay away all day, knowing quite well that he was wanted. I can understand an impetuous decision to keep clear in the hope of getting some quick results, but this – why, it amounts to desertion."

Cortland grunted.

"Is it practicable to put a call out for him, without the Press knowing why?"

Cortland's eyelids looked heavier than usual, and his eyes were dull.

"No," he said flatly. "The story's spreading pretty fast already. Can't expect anything else. Every newspaperman in London was interested in West after the *Witness* pictures, and you can take it from me they know that we're looking for him and that he hasn't reported. Thanked my lucky stars that there was nothing in the evening papers, but there will be in the morning, you can be sure of that."

"So if we put a call out for West, it will not really worsen the situation?"

Cortland considered.

"Wouldn't say that. If I were you, I'd put the call out and say that we're afraid that West has been attacked – he was on a special job, dangerous inquiry, that kind of thing. Even if the Press don't swallow it, they'll have to publish it. Whichever way things turn out, it won't have done any harm."

The Colonel said abruptly: "Very well. See to it, please. I shall be in the office until half-past seven; after that I can be found at my club, and I shall look in at the office before going home. Make sure that the night-duty superintendent knows that, will you?"

"Be staying myself," Cortland said, and got up and went out, rather like a huge bear.

He rubbed his right hand across his forehead as he traipsed along the corridor. He turned into his own office, scowling, and the scowl grew blacker when he saw Sloan, standing by the window, bright-faced and fresh, with his pink-and-white complexion and stiff fair hair.

"Your friend's just about cut his own throat now," he growled, "Why the hell does he have to choose today to behave like a clot?"

Sloan said: "You know him as well as I do."

"Thought I did," grunted Cortland, and dropped down on to his chair. "Thought he had *some* sense." He saw a large envelope on his desk, picked it up, and poked a sharp corner against his chin, as if the slight pain thus caused gave him a little pleasure. "You got any idea what he's really after?"

"Only about this collusion among witnesses."

"Hell of a thing to prove."

"That's what's keeping him."

Cortland shot Sloan a glance from beneath those shaggy eyebrows.

"I told you before, don't be too pro-West over this, keep yourself straight. What do you want?"

"Just came in to see if there was any news."

"There's plenty of news." Cortland picked up a nail-file and used it as a paper-knife to slit open the envelope, which was addressed to him in pencil: *Chief Superintendent Cortland, Scotland Yard.* "Jay's going to put out a general call for West, and now the world will know that he's kicked over the traces. What the hell've we got here?" He looked morosely into the envelope. "Photographs." He shook several prints out on the desk, and they fell face downwards. "Not from our chaps, who'd want—"

He turned the top one over.

He sat there, image-like, his face actually going grey. He didn't move or speak, just sat staring, until Sloan could stand it no longer, and moved and looked over his shoulder.

"My *God!*" Sloan choked.

Cortland's knuckles were white, he was clenching his hands so tightly. Sloan, gritting his teeth, turned the other photographs over. There wasn't much variety except in one; there, a woman was bending over Roger, her lips close to his, her hands cupping his face. The rest were all bedroom scenes. Kate Harrison hadn't a stitch on; nor had Roger, whose hair was tousled, whose eyes were closed.

Cortland said: "Where—" and then shook the envelope savagely. A little slip fell out. He grabbed it. *"The Witness,"* he growled, and Sloan read the words:

With the compliments of The Editor of The Witness

"We've got to kill these," Cortland went on, deep in his throat. "Get me the Editor. *Get a move on!*" His own hand was already on another telephone, and he said "Colonel Jay, quick ... *I said quick* ... I tell you he's in his office; don't keep arguing." He held on, while Sloan got through to the *Witness*, asked for the Editor, and had to hold on. Cortland was still waiting, and placing the photographs in a neat row; Sloan stared at them, shifting his position so that he could see.

"Where the hell's he gone?" Cortland was muttering. "And why don't you get that editor?"

The door opened, and the Assistant Commissioner came in with a brusqueness which was now part of the Yard's routine. Sloan felt himself stiffening to attention.

At the other end of the line, a man said: "Gadding here."

"Superintendent Cortland of New Scotland Yard wishes to speak to you. Will you please—"

"Thought that would shake him," the editor said.

Cortland was getting to his feet, and banging down his telephone.

"Trying to get you, sir. These have—" He swallowed his words, and waved, while the Assistant Commissioner reached a spot from where he could see all the pictures. "These have just come in."

"He's on the line," Sloan said.

Cortland took the telephone. "Cortland here. Thanks for the pictures." It must have cast him a big effort to sound so unconcerned. "Weren't planning to use them, were you?"

He stood there listening.

The Assistant Commissioner was looking down at the photographs, and Sloan could see his jaws working, could see the glitter in his eyes. Cortland was still listening. Sloan wished himself in another part of the world, but had to wait and see this through.

"All right; who's talking about pressure?" Cortland demanded. "I'm just warning you that if you print those photographs and they prove to be faked, we'll have the skin off your back. Hold on a minute; here's the Assistant Commissioner." He hugged the mouthpiece close to his chest, and looked at Jay as if he didn't care whether Jay was the Home Secretary himself. "He says he's going to use the two that are half decent, and nothing we can say will stop him. Only hope we've got is to make him leery in case they're faked. Sloan!" Cortland was now the leading authority and Jay didn't try to interrupt. "Get those blasted pictures up to the Photography Room, tell whoever's on duty we want reasonable evidence they could be faked. And ring me the minute he's got any kind of report. You agree, sir?"

"You handle it," Jay conceded.

"Listen, Mr. Gadding," Cortland said into the telephone. "It's my considered opinion that these photographs are faked, and if you use them you do so on your own responsibility. And if they backfire …" Obviously the editor interrupted him. Cortland glowered at Jay, as if it was his fault. Then: "Well, if you're sure they're not faked, use them and be damned to you, but there's something else … Where did you get them? … You sure? … Listen, Gadding; if this is another put-up job like the one last night … So you don't think that was put-up, don't you? You'll learn, and if you take a tip from me you'll cut out this hostile stuff, and take a new angle – be on our side for once." Unexpectedly, he grinned. "All right, ta. 'Bye."

He rang off.

Jay waited for an explanation, without speaking.

"He says he had an anonymous call to send a photographer to Mrs. Harrison's place, and did so. A boy let the photographer in. He also says he'll keep them out of the early editions, and if we can prove they're faked, he'll keep them out altogether," Cortland said. "Otherwise, he'll use them. He's been on to the paper's Managing Director, who agrees. Their duty to clean up the Yard, that kind of tripe, but it can look good in headlines."

Cortland stopped, and swallowed hard, as if he just realised that he had been talking to Jay as if Jay was a junior.

Jay said: "Cortland, have you any reason to believe those pictures are faked?"

"Can't believe they're not," Cortland growled. "They look real enough to me, but if we can find a way of keeping them out of the *Witness* it'll give us time to think."

"If that is the kind of behaviour that a senior officer at Scotland Yard indulges in, then perhaps it will do the Force good, not harm, if the pictures are published. Perhaps if the scandal goes deeply enough, it will be possible to get the fullest possible co-operation from all ranks."

Each word was the slash of a whip.

"You can actually make out the window-frames and a door-handle; obviously there were taken furtively," Jay went on.

The door opened as he finished, and Sloan came in with the pictures. The Colonel did not glance round, but looked as if he was trying to quell any resistance.

"If those pictures are published, we'll be right down the drain," Sloan said gruffly. "They're genuine as far as it goes, but—"

"If those pictures are published it will awaken the conscience of the Force," Jay barked.

"If those pictures are published, and we could have prevented it, I'll be finished with the Force." Sloan's chin was thrust forward and his eyes glittered as he drew nearer. "It's time someone put in a word for West, sir, and time you realised that if West had believed he could obtain the co-operation he ought to be able to rely on from here, we wouldn't be in any trouble. He's been out on a job. He's been as worried as hell because he knows that he's being shot at. He's got the best brain at the Yard, bar none, and he's got more guts than any two of the rest of us put together. Do you think he doesn't know what risk he's been taking? Don't you realise that he's putting the job first and himself afterwards? He could have stayed here, yes-sirring and no-sirring, getting himself in good while he was falling down on the job. So he's chosen the hard way. Why don't you get behind him? Why don't you listen to the evidence of ten years of results, ten years while he's worked himself to a standstill just to make sure he always gets the right man? If he can take risks for it, if he'll stick his neck out for the job and for the Yard, how about the Yard getting behind him? Those photographs aren't faked, but they're phoney. I've known West and his wife and family for over ten years, and I tell you West wouldn't get into bed with another woman. He's in love with his wife, and the only trouble he's ever had with her is when he's put the Yard first. More than once it came damned near to wrecking his home." When neither of the others responded, and even the Colonel seemed taken aback, Sloan went on roundly: "Look at these photographs again. Did you ever see a man hold a woman like that? His hands were placed there. He was doped when that picture was taken, and didn't know a thing about it. Why don't we find out who the woman is, and get moving? If we can prove those pictures are faked or taken when West was doped, we can stop the *Witness* printing them, we could even make them destroy a whole edition. How about fighting for West, instead of sticking a knife in our own man's back?"

Chapter Eighteen

Waking

Roger struggled up in bed.

His head felt as if it was splitting, and there was a sharp pain as well as a weight at his eyes. His limbs felt sluggish, too. He knew that he was in an unfamiliar place, but at first he did not recollect where. As he struggled up, something shimmered a little in front of his eyes, and he saw that they were photographs of some kind, but it didn't strike him as strange.

He pushed a pillow behind his back.

This was a woman's room. It was small, there was some good furniture, the thick carpet was fitted from wall to wall. On the mantelpiece there was the photograph of a man he didn't know, another of a boy, a third of a woman.

Then he remembered.

Kate Harrison, and her Clive.

He felt himself shiver, uncontrollably. He looked down at his bare chest and flat stomach, and in that moment realised exactly what had happened. He pressed a hand against his forehead, and for a few moments the pain seemed to get worse. Then he took his hand away, could see better, and could look at the facts without that searing pain.

There were the glossy photographs.

He picked the nearest one up.

He needed only to see that one to discover just how tightly he was caught. He seemed to concentrate on it for a long time, then glanced swiftly at the others, flung them aside, and jumped out of bed. His clothes were in a heap on an upright chair against the wall. He put them on, quickly. It was warm in the room, and the effort made him sweat, but in a way that did him good. He had shaken off the inertia of those first few paralysing minutes. He stuffed his tie in his pocket as he strode towards the door. It wouldn't have surprised him to find it locked, but it was open. He stepped on to the landing, and listened, heard a sound of voices, and couldn't be sure whose. He hurried down the stairs, with much of his usual briskness.

A shadow appeared from the kitchen.

"You lousy swine," a lad said.

This was Clive Harrison, standing there with his fists clenched and chin thrust forward; an outraged hero. He was undoubtedly a handsome kid. Roger turned towards him, and he stood his ground. Behind him, standing in the kitchen with a dishcloth in her hand, was Kate Harrison; she wore a high-necked apron over the dress she'd worn at tea.

"You're not going to touch her again," Clive said viciously. "Why, I'd rather—"

Roger didn't stop Clive striking out, but caught his wrist, twisted slightly, and threw him heavily against the wall with a judo hold that took the boy completely by surprise. Clive didn't try again. Kate stood with the tea-towel drooping from her hand, her mouth open, scared-looking.

"All right," Roger said. "I'm not going to wring your neck. Who put you up to this? Pegg or your lodger Sydney?" He kept moving forward. "Come on, who—"

Syd appeared from a door beyond the kitchen. He was in his shirt sleeves, and wore a belt, not braces. He was chewing rhythmically, but with very slight movements of his cheeks and mouth.

"So you think you can talk your way out of this," he said, and looked Roger up and down mockingly. "You took Kate upstairs with you, and told her that was the only way she could keep you quiet.

You made her believe you had evidence which could put her inside. So she gave in."

"Rotten liar," Clive said, from behind Roger.

"I can put her inside all right," Roger said. "I can put all three of you inside. You lunatic, you've done the one thing needed to prove I was right."

The woman caught her breath.

For a moment, Syd stopped chewing. His dark eyes seemed to glow, the muscles of his brown forearms twitched a little, and that was all. Clive didn't speak, but Roger saw him moving forward, and realised that he was as startled as the others.

"Just talk," Syd sneered at last, and went on chewing.

"You can't see the nose on your face," Roger jeered. "The rest of the world might not know it yet, but I know you framed me. There might be some at the Yard who won't want to believe it, but there'll be a damned sight more who'll know this couldn't be true. They'll know that if you framed me, there's a good reason to think you framed Quist." He looked searingly from Syd to the woman then to Clive. "There isn't one of you with a chance. You'll get a lifer, Sydney. Kate will get ten years as accessory, and as for you—" He swung round on Clive, and the lad started back. "You'll get the next four or five years in a reform school. You and your fine intellect, you and your clever ideas. You haven't any more sense than a ten-year-old girl; she wouldn't be so crazy as this."

Syd had stopped chewing again.

"Talk," he said, but the word didn't come easily.

Kate spun round on him. "Syd, does he mean it? Can he do it—"

"He hasn't got a chance!"

"Listen to me, Kate," Roger said savagely. "Before I came here I was prepared to believe that you'd been terrorised into saying what Syd and Pegg told you. I thought you'd probably persuaded your son to lie, for the same reason. Well, I know better now. You must have been in it from the beginning; you're guilty of being accessory after the fact of your own sister's murder, and nothing can keep you out of jail, except—"

He broke off and glowered at them. None of them said a word.

"You'd better buy some legal advice," he rasped. "I won't give it to you free."

He swung round, and the boy moved quickly, as if half scared. Roger went along the narrow passage to the door. He could hear the others' laboured breathing; it wouldn't have surprised him had the woman cried out, but she did not. He opened the street door, and stepped into the evening air. It was still bright daylight, at nearly nine o'clock. Across the road was a young detective officer from the Yard, a thin, dark-haired man, not the one who had been on duty earlier. Roger beckoned him, while standing with his back to the open door. He heard whispering behind him, and knew that the woman and the boy were very uneasy.

The D.O. glanced swiftly up and down the road, and ran across, just beating a bus which made the door quiver in Roger's hand as it passed.

"Mr. West!"

"That's right," said Roger. "I want—"

"I've just had a message that Mr. Sloan is on his way here, sir. He should turn up any minute."

"Fine. Get round to the back of this place." Roger spoke in a clear voice which those behind him could not fail to hear: "If you pick up a constable or so on the way, better do it. You might run into a man with a knife. Be careful."

"I'll watch it, sir." The D.O. turned and ran towards the nearest corner; obviously he knew how to get to the back. Roger looked up and down the road, hoping desperately that Sloan wouldn't be long, trying not to think beyond the urgent need for action. Buses and cyclists and one or two small cars were in sight, but no other traffic. He turned towards the front door. Clive and his mother were still there, in the kitchen doorway at the end of a passage alongside the stairs, but there was no sign of Syd.

Clive looked scared.

Roger didn't speak. Kate Harrison came forward with a hand pressed tight against her breast, and said hoarsely: "I didn't know anything about it, I didn't do anything."

"So you didn't do anything," Roger echoed icily. "You let them turn your only son into a liar and a criminal, you make as sure as anyone can that he'll spend most of his life in jail, and now you start squealing. Once a kid starts on this road, he doesn't get off it easily."

She was gasping for breath. "I didn't mean—"

Clive's defiance had wilted, and he stood looking a helpless and bewildered child.

"I—I didn't mean to," Kate said in that hoarse voice. "They made me do it; I was frightened of them. They had me scared stiff, can't you see? How—how can I put it right?" Her fear made her pathetic; perhaps only now had she realised the inevitable results of what she had been doing. "Mr. West, tell me how I can put it right."

Then Roger saw terror take the place of fear, in her eyes, terror of someone behind him. It was the change in her expression which saved him. He spun round. He saw two men, both strangers, creeping from the porch towards him. In one man's hand was a black-jack, in another a brass knuckle-duster.

Roger had a split second's warning.

He shouted: "Police! Police!" and leapt at the man with the cosh. There was no time for half-measures, hardly time to save himself. He planted his foot in the man's stomach and thrust him backwards, then half turned towards the one with the knuckle-duster, who was striking out. He felt the harsh scrape of the brass on the side of his jaw. The pain made him wince, but he had time to drive his clenched fist into the man's stomach, all his strength behind it. Now he had them both off balance, but that wasn't the thing that mattered most: he had to get back into the house.

The door slammed.

"Come and help!" he roared. "Help!"

Two youths paused on the other side of the road, but made no move. A girl on a bicycle pulled up sharply, making the brakes squeal. A bus lumbered by, vibrating, several passengers staring. No other men were near at hand. The two men whom Roger had beaten off came at him again, one from each side, and this time it wasn't going to be easy, although his back was to the closed front door.

He heard a scream from behind it.

He heard Kate scream: "No, no, no!"

He heard the boy shout.

Then he was in the middle of the fight again, felt the cosh in a slicing blow just above his right ear, and the knuckle-duster smack into his chest; it hurt badly but didn't put him down.

The two youths were coming across at last, running, shouting. One of Roger's assailants turned; Roger dodged the other and hooked the first man's legs from under him. He felt another savage blow on the shoulder, but it was the last. The two youths came on in a running tackle, and brought the man down.

Roger was gasping for breath.

"Hold—hold them," he gasped, and turned towards the door, thrusting his injured shoulder at it, and clenching his teeth against the pain. The door wouldn't budge. He heard a groaning sound, that was all; no screaming, no shouting, just groaning. He drew back and flung his weight wildly against the door, but still it didn't budge. Then he heard a car pull up, and out of the corner of his eye he saw men spilling out of it; Sloan was among them.

"Must get in!" Roger bellowed. "Hurry!"

He jumped towards the window of the room where he'd had tea, bent his elbow and cracked it through the glass. As he did so, Sloan and another man reached him, and Sloan said: "Take a spell."

He pushed Roger aside roughly. Roger watched him and the other man knock the slivers of glass out from the sides of the windows, and saw Sloan climb through. As he went, Roger said in that gasping voice: "Check the back, too. Are there enough men?"

Sloan bellowed an order to two men who were tackling Roger's assailants.

"One of you go round the back."

"Right, sir!"

"You radioed for more men?"

"Yes."

So this part of it was over bar shouting, Roger realised, and in that moment he felt weak and useless. His legs were heavy, he didn't want to climb in at the window, and there was no need. Sloan was half-way in, his man was already right inside the room. Roger caught a glimpse of the tea-table, just as he had last seen it, and then turned towards the front door. One of the three men who had come with Sloan was fastening handcuffs on to each of the assailants and a little ring of people was standing some way off. The two youths who had run to help were sidling towards the crowd, each wearing Edwardian-style suits, each obviously a Teddy boy, each a little sheepish.

"Take their names," Roger called, "They ought to get a medal, and I want to buy them a drink." He flashed his smile, although it was real physical effort, saw three uniformed policemen hurrying, and knew that there was nothing else to worry about outside.

But inside?

He heard footsteps. The moaning had stopped, and he tried to tell himself that was a good sign. He longed for the door to open, but it didn't, for what seemed a long time. He raised his voice: "Bill, open up!"

Then the door opened, and Roger could see inside.

Kate Harrison lay in a peculiar position close to the wall, and her son at the foot of the stairs.

Both were dead; stabbed to death.

Sloan was standing up from the woman's side, but there was no need for a doctor to come, save that of formality. The other Yard man was out of sight. The doors leading to the back yard were wide open, and Roger could see a tall oblong of daylight there. He exchanged glances with Sloan, then hurried along the passage, through the kitchen, into the yard. At the small gate at one end, leading to a service alley, the man he had sent round in the beginning lay on the ground; he had been knifed too. The detective officer was kneeling by his side, and he looked round desperately.

"Ambulance, quick."

Roger nodded, and ran back into the house. It would be quicker to dial 999 than to go to the car radio, for there were too many people outside. Sloan was closing the door, and he turned as Roger lifted the receiver.

"I've sent for a doctor."

"Ambulance?"

"That can wait."

"Not when you've seen our man at the back door," Roger said, and when he heard the operator, asked for the Yard, and gave the order ...

He put the receiver down slowly, squared his shoulders, looked at Kate Harrison and her son, and felt as if he was going to choke. He found a cigarette, from Sloan, in his hand, a lighter flaming steadily in front of him. He stared at Sloan for what seemed a long time, then suddenly said: "Damned fool!" and snatched up the receiver again and dialled the Yard. "Hallo, Abbott; it's West here again. Put out calls for the following men: First: Theophilus Pegg, Warehouseman of Henrietta Street, Covent Garden; see his description in the Jensen file on my desk. Second: Man named Sydney, Christian name not certain, of 101 Hadworth Palace Road, aged about forty, dark brown eyes, thin dark hair, thin face, sallow complexion, tight lips, small scar below right eye just above cheekbone, medium height, carrying a knife and known to be dangerous. Chews gum freely. Third: Charles Henry, of—"

"We know Henry," the *Information Room* man said. "Been busy, Handsome?"

"Yes, and also pick up Mrs. Kimmeridge, of 31 Page Street, Elwell."

"Right. You know that Jay's after you?"

"Yes, thanks," Roger said. "Send word that I'm coming, will you?"

Chapter Nineteen

Report To Jay

Colonel Jay sat at his desk, and the light from a single lamp above his head shone on him, showing his features in sharp relief, revealing the tautness of his mouth and the way his eyes were narrowed. His arms were on the sides of his chair, the hands lightly clenched. On his right, a little way from the desk, sat Cortland. The blinds were down at the windows, and this room seemed cut off from the rest of the world.

Roger saw all this as he stepped inside.

He would not have been surprised had he been given an escort from the time he had stepped into the Yard, but nothing of the kind had happened. He had telephoned Cortland, been told to wait in his office, then been summoned here. There had been time to have an antiseptic dabbed on his chest and chin where the knuckle-duster had scraped, and one deep scratch was covered with plaster.

He did not know that his eyes looked unnaturally bright and that his expression was at least as bleak as the Assistant Commissioner's.

He did not know what to expect, beyond immediate suspension, had no idea how Jay would receive him. His nerves were at their rawest. He had been fighting with himself all the way to the office, telling himself that he must keep calm, that he must take whatever Jay wanted to hand out. He couldn't expect Jay to let it go formally, certainly couldn't expect him to understand what tension he had lived through in the past hour or so.

Jay waited for him to speak.

"Good evening, sir. I've come to report."

If Jay was sarcastic, or if he delivered a withering rebuke—

"I would like you to confine your report to briefest outline," Jay said. His tone was flat and unemotional.

"Very good, sir." That was a start, but the rest wasn't so easy. It had been a long day. For the moment Roger couldn't recall exactly how it had started; he had a kind of mental black-out, and his legs felt weak. That must be the effect of the drug. Here he was, with a chance to put his case plainly and crisply; and here he was, standing like a schoolboy. Clive Harrison. Clive, with his throat cut. He could picture the mother and son on the floor, and in his ears there was Kate Harrison's screaming. *No, no, no, no.*

She had seen death coming.

Cortland's big hands moved, as he fidgeted with unaccustomed embarrassment.

Roger began.

"Briefly then, sir, I had reason to doubt the statements of some witnesses, and to suspect collusion among them. The form of collusion suggested that they were either desperate, hardly knowing what to say next, or were playing for time. The second possibility made it a matter of extreme urgency to find out the truth. I soon found indications that at least two of the witnesses against Michael Quist were untrustworthy."

Roger paused, and moistened his lips. He could have done with a drink, and the carafe of water and the glass on Jay's desk seemed to mock him. He could do with a chair, too, but he stood stiffly in front of the Assistant Commissioner, who watched him steadily – coldly.

"I came to the conclusion that it would be impracticable to pass the information on to other officers, which would be necessary if I returned here, sir. I had no formal evidence, no justification for charging any of the people concerned, but I believed that if it were possible to get one or all of the witnesses agitated and on the run, quick results might be achieved. On the other hand, if they had time to consolidate their position, they might be able to substantiate their false evidence against Quist. I decided that I had to work fast and alone. Finally I visited a sister of the dead woman, the mother of the boy, Clive Harrison. While there, I accepted some tea and cake. It was drugged."

He paused again.

Here was an opportunity for Jay to be really withering. Why had he eaten anything at the house, why had he had even a cup of tea? Could he *prove* that he had been drugged?

There were the photographs on the desk; no one could be blamed for believing their evidence.

Jay said: "Continue, please."

"When I came round, I found that evidence had been faked against me, in the way I believed it had been faked against Quist. Mrs. Harrison, her son and a man named Sydney were still in the house. Mrs. Harrison was extremely nervous and likely to make a statement if she was subjected to sufficient close questioning. I did not know that two other men, associates of Sydney, were on the spot. When I went outside for help, they attacked me. Sydney closed the front door, shutting them and me out in the street. I heard the woman and the boy scream. Mrs. Harrison and her son each died of knife-wounds." Roger paused, and then added briefly: "In outline, that's it, sir. I don't yet know the whole story."

Why didn't Jay say something? Why did he sit there like some shrivelled-up relic of the Poona days? It was obvious that he would suspend Roger pending the investigation; why didn't he get on with it?

Jay said: "Theophilus Pegg and Mrs. Kimmeridge are in the waiting-rooms here, and Charles Henry should be on his way. Is it your intention to interview them yourself, or to leave their interrogation to others?"

What was this?

Is it *your* intention—

"I think someone much fresher than I am ought to question them, sir; two of them especially are very shrewd customers. The most likely one to break down is Charles Henry."

"Was it your intention to prefer charges?"

"I meant to apply at once for search warrants for all their places of business and residence, and charge them if reasonable grounds for such charges were found, sir. Failing a charge, I would detain each of them all night and release them in the morning, under close surveillance."

"I see." Jay turned to Cortland. "Do you agree with that course, Superintendent?"

"Yeh," said Cortland.

"Very well. Put everything in hand, please. West, I would like you to report to me here at ten o'clock in the morning; until then you are to remain off duty."

Roger said: "Very well, sir," and found himself adding: "Thank you."

"He's a devil, but probably a fair devil," Cortland said to Roger as they walked along the corridor. "Let's hope so, anyhow. Get a car to drive you home, and tuck in early. Shouldn't even go into your office again."

"Oh, I'd like to see what's there," Roger said. "Coming?"

Cortland followed him.

There were several reports, including one from Ibbetson about Henry being at the Rose and Crown on Monday night. The one man who swore Henry had been there all the time was a barman named Sydney.

It was the same Sydney, and that smashed Henry's alibi completely.

Roger grinned as he handed the report to Cortland.

"See that? Once Henry cracks—"

He stopped.

Sloan came hurrying into the C.I.'s office, and he never moved at that speed for the sake of it; moreover, he had been on duty since eight o'clock that morning.

"Trouble out at Hadworth," he said curtly. "Henry went out of his house, and someone attacked him."

Roger dropped the report as if his life depended on it. "Corty, I'm taking a car to North Hadworth; you can't keep me out of this," he said. He strode towards the lift, and didn't see the exasperation on Cortland's face gradually change to a reluctant grin.

"I'll put out the call, you go with him," Cortland said to Sloan. "Get a move on."

Sybil Henry and her mother had been sitting in the front room of the house when the telephone call had come. Charles Henry had been in the dining-room, ostensibly reading, probably just sitting. He had refused to speak to Sybil, had repeatedly ordered her to get out of his house, once or twice had rounded on his wife for encouraging her to remain. Now he seemed to have accepted the fact that she would stay, but he kept out of her way.

Sybil saw the way her mother winced when the telephone bell rang. They heard Henry move very quickly, heard him pluck up the instrument, and say: "Yes, Henry speaking."

There was a brief pause; then: "All right," he said.

Mrs. Henry leaned across to her daughter and put a hand on her knee.

"He—he's going out *again*. In spite of all that's happened, he's going out again." It was like a sob.

Sybil said very softly: "Yes, he is, and this time he *isn't* going to see Rose Jensen, is he?" She sat there with the light shining on her clear eyes and her flawless face, and there was doubt and uncertainty in her expression. She stood up, slowly.

"Sybil," her mother gasped, "you're not to go out!"

"I won't be long," Sybil said, and pressed her mother's shoulder gently. "There's no need to worry; that detective's still outside."

Her mother said brokenly: "If only I knew what it was about, if only I could help him."

Sybil went to the door.

Her father was coming down the stairs. He was staring straight ahead, and she didn't think that he saw her. His footsteps were very heavy, and he put a hand on the banisters, as if he needed their support. He went straight to the front door, put on his bowler hat, and stepped out; the door closed behind him with a snap.

It was dusk.

Sybil went out, hatless, coatless, into the warm evening and the scented garden. She heard someone cutting a lawn in spite of the near darkness, and saw her father's heavy figure, close to the gate. She couldn't see the detective, but felt sure that he was there, and that he would follow her father. She heard the slight squeak of the gate opening, and saw her father step outside.

Then she saw another man, lurking in the clump of rhododendron bushes inside the garden and close to the gate. She fancied that she saw something glint in his hand.

She screamed.

Henry began to swing round, clumsily. Sybil ran towards the gate, as the man from the bushes leapt at her father. Someone shouted not far off, and heavy footsteps sounded on the road.

The lawn-mower stopped.

Sybil heard her father cry out, as if in pain, and saw him strike wildly at the man from the bushes. Then he grappled with the man. They were swaying when the detective from the road came rushing up, and the man who had attacked her father turned and ran.

He came straight at her.

She could see the way his lips were parted and his teeth glinted. She saw his sallow face and shimmering eyes. She saw the knife in his hand, although it no longer glinted; it was dark red. She did not think that there was a chance to avoid him. The running detective had collided with her father, but she didn't see that; she stayed as if hypnotised in front of the man with the knife.

From behind her, her mother screamed: *"Sybil!"*

The shriek must have distracted the man; he missed a step and wavered. Sybil flung herself to one side as he recovered and came on. She did not see him leap into the shrubbery at one side of the house, or climb the wall into a neighbour's garden. She only knew that he had gone, that her mother was rushing up, that her father lay on the ground, that neighbours were hurrying towards him, and that the big detective was racing in the direction of the escaping man.

Roger reached Laurel Avenue less than twenty minutes after the incident. He had picked up a general report on the car radio, but did not know how Henry was, or whether Sybil had been hurt. He saw a big white ambulance outside the house, with the inevitable crowd being kept on the move by the inevitable policeman in blue. The driver pulled up twenty yards away from the people on the fringe, and he and Sloan jumped out of the back. They saw Henry on a stretcher, being pushed into the ambulance.

"Face not covered, so he's alive," Sloan observed.

"Can't all go wrong," Roger said. "I'll give ten to one Sydney came out here to cut Henry's throat, too." He climbed a wooden fence in the next-door garden, so that he could get to Sybil and her mother, who were standing with friends by the gate. Detective Sergeant Ibbetson was near them with a Divisional man.

Ibbetson spotted Roger in the gloom, and came hurrying.

"Could kick myself all the way to the Yard for this, sir. Chap must have crept through the next-door garden. I hadn't any idea he was there until I heard Miss Henry scream."

"How's Henry?"

"Knife-wounds in the stomach and side, sir; touch and go, I think."

"Anyone else hurt?"

"No, thank God."

"Get a good look at the fellow?"

"Good enough, I think; he answered the description of the man Sydney. There's a call out for him."

"What's been done?"

"Whole district is alerted, and the neighbouring Divisions warned," said the Divisional man, a little diffidently. "We'll get him before long, Mr. West."

"He's a sight too slippery for my liking," Roger growled. "Bill, get that car turned round; we want to go to Page Street."

"But he wouldn't be crazy enough to go there!"

"He probably doesn't know we've picked Mrs. K. up yet; he might have a cut at her," Roger said. "I'll be with you in a couple of jiffs." He went nearer to the gate, as the ambulance drove off. Sybil stood with her arm at her mother's waist, and neighbours hung about, with the helpless goodwill of such occasions.

Roger said: "Did your father tell you where he was going, Miss Henry?"

She looked at him almost wearily.

"He had a telephone call, and went straight out," she said, and then a little life sparked in her eyes. "And this time it couldn't have been to see Rose Jensen, could it? Mr. West, perhaps my father didn't—"

"We're finding out," Roger said quietly. "Telephone me if there is anything I can do."

She nodded.

Roger doubted whether her mother had understood anything he had said. He turned and hurried back to the car, where the driver was already at the wheel with the engine ticking over. There wasn't must likelihood of finding Sydney at Page Street, but it was worth a try.

"Anything else on your mind?" Sloan asked, almost humbly.

"We've got search-parties at Pegg's office and home, and at Page Street. Kate Harrison's place will have been turned inside out by now, and Sydney lived there, remember. We've been through Quist's place. The one place we haven't access to yet is Henry's bank."

"You'll need dynamite to get anything done there before the morning."

"Yes," Roger agreed, "and we may have to get some. Take a straight look at it, Bill. This man Sydney killed the Harrisons almost in front of my eyes. He must know that he can't get away with it, *or* else he's sure that he can. If he feels sure that he can, then something's laid on for him to get out of London, perhaps out of the country, tonight. So we'll watch all airports and seaports and main-line railway termini. That's the routine. But why did Sydney think it worth that desperate chance to kill Kate Harrison and the boy? Why did he take another chance, and come to kill Henry? What makes him so desperate? What makes it worth his while?"

Sloan said: "Search me."

"There must be a reason. The obvious one is to keep their mouths shut. He may have get-away plans they knew about, and he may even be trying to protect someone else. He'd only do that if it paid off well."

Sloan actually caught his breath.

"Any idea who?"

"We could have a lead," Roger said, and there was fierce excitement in his voice. "The puzzling thing has been Samuelson's effort to keep back evidence in Quist's favour, hasn't it? It doesn't fit into anything we yet know. I thought it was a smart way of handling Quist's defence, a way I couldn't follow. But supposing he *wants* Quist blamed? He works for Saxby's, so he's doing this for a Saxby big shot. Is it someone who's been in this from the beginning, who knew it would be found out eventually, and wanted someone else to take the blame?"

"Well, who?"

"A certain Mr. Gorringe, who denied having received Quist's report, and who put Samuelson on the job," Roger said softly. "Gorringe knew we were bound to catch up eventually with trouble at Saxby's; it would suit him nicely to have a stooge sitting in for him. And by trying to investigate on his own, Quist would fit in perfectly."

"Gorringe," breathed Sloan.

They turned into Page Street. Two plainclothes men were standing together near Number 31, and a uniformed constable was walking along the other side of the street, all of them clear in the street lamps, and the last tinge of the afterglow; a peaceful scene.

"Stop a minute, driver." Roger waited impatiently until the car had pulled in, and leaned over the back of the empty seat next to the driver, for the radio telephone; he switched it on. "Give me the Night Superintendent," he said, and went on talking to Sloan; "Gorringe is in a perfect position to defraud Saxby's in a big way. The firm's secretary is away, and Gorringe is in full charge of the financial side for three months – time to racket a fortune in a bank account as large as Saxby's. So …" He broke off, as a man with a slightly north-country accent sounded over the air, "Hallo, is that Superintendent Thwaites? … Yes, West here. Charley, Saxby's ran their own air freight to the Continent and Africa, don't they? …

Using Croydon airport these days, I think. It's possible that Sydney's making for Croydon airport, and that he'll try to board a Saxby plane leaving the country tonight. Will you cover it? ... Fine, and there's another thing. It might help if we can check the bank where Henry worked, try and prise some bank officials out, will you?" He rang off, smiling tautly, and Sloan saw the glint in his eyes and marvelled; for Roger West looked as fresh as if he'd just had a full night's sleep.

Roger switched off the radio.

"Where now?" Sloan demanded. "Croydon or the bank?"

"Croydon," Roger said.

Chapter Twenty

Airport

There were dozens of lights at the airport, and the sound of at least two engines warming up. As Roger's car swung towards the runways, waved on by airport officials who had been warned to expect them, he saw two men approaching a small aircraft some distance away. Car headlamps were turned towards these men, who were looking round. They were too far away for him to recognise them, but he saw the name *Saxby's* on the side of the craft they were approaching. Other police cars were already waiting, and Roger saw at least two on the far side of the field.

The mechanics were ready to take away the chocks from the Saxby aircraft. Once the two men got aboard, they wouldn't have a chance, of course, for the pilot would be stopped. That was why the police cars were holding off.

Then Roger recognised one of the men as he reached the steps leading to the aircraft's cabin. It was Sydney, who turned round and seemed to hesitate. Sydney spoke to the second man, who pointed to the cabin doorway, and started up the steps.

Sydney didn't.

He turned, suddenly, and began to run. He went swiftly, and obviously headed for the fence at the side of the great field, certainly hoping to climb it and get away among the warrens of streets and tiny houses. Whatever else he lacked, he had guts.

The other man was standing hesitantly on the steps.

Now the police moved.

Two cars headed for the aircraft, and two for Sydney. Roger said jerkily: "After the running man." It should have been easy, but it wasn't. Two petrol tankers, a firefighting unit and several stacks of freight and luggage were in the way, preventing a clear run. For a moment Sydney disappeared; then he came in sight, running desperately towards the fence. Roger's driver swung the car in the same direction, and stepped on the accelerator. The car raced forward, but it couldn't go at speed for long. Just ahead was a wire fence round an enclosure which the driver hadn't noticed.

He jammed on his brakes.

Roger rasped: "Come on," and opened the door as the car slowed down. He heard Sloan yell, but ignored him. He jumped out, kept his balance and leapt over the enclosure fence. Sydney was only fifty yards away, and equidistant from the main fence which he was so anxious to reach. He didn't seem to have seen Roger, and when he twisted round he was looking only at the pursuing cars.

Sloan was pounding behind Roger.

Suddenly, Sydney turned, and saw them as their shadows were cast long and dark by the lamps of the stranded car. Sydney probably didn't know who they were, but any policeman was a danger to him then.

He flung out his right arm.

"He's got a gun!" Sloan shouted. "Look out!"

Roger didn't swerve, didn't slacken speed, put everything he had into racing towards Sydney. If the man once got away, he might stay in hiding for a long time; might even live to kill again and again.

Sydney paused, to turn and fire, but he didn't give himself enough time to steady his aim. Roger saw the flash of the shot, but didn't know where the bullet went. He was only five yards away, and another shot might be fatal; next time he would have to dodge. He saw Sydney stop again and level the gun.

Then Sydney kicked against something on the ground, and pitched headlong. His gun fell from his grasp, and when Roger reached him, he was dazed, helpless and unarmed.

The other man, now held by the police, was Gorringe of Saxby's. The police boarded the waiting aircraft, and found twenty-one thousand pounds, stolen that day from Henry's bank, undoubtedly by Henry himself, as well as securities and records of large credits in overseas banks, enough to have kept a dozen men for years.

"Well, it was simpler than it looked," Roger said, when they were back at the Yard. "Gorringe caved in when we caught him, and talked. He was in it from the start, and it began with Pegg's. He'd allowed Pegg's to overcharge for years, and taken a cut. Then they both grew greedier, and worked the same trick with some associated companies. But it wasn't big money. When Saxby's secretary went on a long visit to the United States and left Gorringe in charge, it looked a perfect opportunity. They began some cheque fiddles, but not until they'd got Henry under their thumb. First he was involved with Rose Jensen – Pegg's cousin – and she became his mistress. Being a bank official, and banks being notorious for disliking any employee to create a scandal, they had a good hold on him. Then they bribed him with a cut in the proceeds. He passed forged and altered cheques, and sometimes paid out big cash sums. He was frequently told that it wouldn't last much longer, and led by the nose to a big robbery, like last night's. By then he believed he could be found guilty of murder, and daren't back out. He was telephoned about a job on the night that he was followed by Quist, and Rose Jensen was murdered. He saw Rose to plead with her to help him get free of the stranglehold. Rose knew everyone involved, and knew that Henry was desperate enough to kill himself. She phoned Sydney and threatened to squeal if they didn't stop the pressure – so she had to be killed.

"One of Pegg's men, a motor-cyclist named Chick, followed Henry, and saw Quist already following the man. Quist was a thorn in their flesh, but Gorringe had known what he was doing for some time – and Gorringe knew that when Saxby's secretary came back the frauds would be found out. So he let Quist go on probing – and planned to frame him as the murderer.

"No one but Pegg knew that Gorringe was the Saxby end of the racket, and as Quist became dangerous, Gorringe and Pegg prepared what looked like a masterly coup. Quist was to be framed, and take the rap for Gorringe; the police would get on to Quist, Henry, Sydney and the others, but Pegg was to try to keep in the clear by a simple double-cross.

"He and Gorringe were all ready to take the first good chance. It came when Sydney telephoned Pegg and reported Rose Jensen's threat, and added that Quist had followed Henry to Rose's place. Pegg told Sydney to kill Rose and frame Quist. Sydney jumped at what seemed a chance to put himself in the clear.

"But he very soon began to see the snags. He tried to have Quist killed by Chick, but that failed. Pegg kept him reasonably sweet by promising the world. Pegg himself planned to leave the country in a Saxby plane, with a good share of the money that Henry was to steal – and he would stay away until it all blew over."

Roger paused, and Cortland grunted.

"Didn't expect Sydney to let him get away with a double-cross, did he?"

"He did, and he was right," Roger went on. "If Quist was successfully framed for the murder, Sydney would just go down for a few years. But if Quist wasn't framed, Sydney would get a lifer, even if he wasn't hanged. Kate Harrison and the boy were on Pegg's side – Pegg paid them well to make sure of that.

"Then Ibbetson discovered the relationship between Rose Jensen and Pegg, and that started the rot," Roger went on. "Pegg had to play for time enough for Henry to finish his job and get the cash, and Sydney had to be kept quiet. But Sydney was suspicious already.

"Both Pegg and Gorringe realised that the only hope left was flight – or we would catch up with them both. Pegg told Kate he was planning to get away – he had to, so as to keep her quiet. When the lid blew off at Kate's house tonight, she almost certainly tried to save herself by telling Sydney about the get-away. Once he knew that, Sydney killed her and the boy because they could warn us about the airfield. Then he tried to kill Henry – who also knew. Next he went to the airfield in place of Pegg—"

"What kept Pegg away?" demanded Cortland.

"Sydney telephoned him and threatened to kill him if he went near the airfield, and Pegg took that seriously," Roger answered. "Obviously, Sydney's only hope was flight. What would have happened if he and Gorringe had got away is anybody's guess. He might have cooled down or might have murdered Gorringe at the first opportunity. That would have been killing the goose which laid the golden eggs – only Gorringe and Pegg could get at the money planted in banks in many parts of Africa."

"Question's irrelevant," Cortland said gruffly. "Damned clever scheme. We could easily have proved a case against Quist. I suppose Gorringe took that report of Quist's."

"Yes. And burned it," Roger said.

"Did Henry think Quist was the Saxby end of the racket?" Cortland asked,

"He did, from the time he realised that Quist had been in Page Street on the night of the murder," Roger said. "He couldn't have named either Gorringe or Pegg – only Sydney. As it is, no one can put a finger on Samuelson, but we will one day." He checked a yawn.

"Time you went home," Cortland declared. "You've had quite a day."

Janet opened the front door of the house in Bell Street, and saw Roger step out of the police car which had brought him home. It was nearly half-past twelve. She came hurrying, a sure indication of anxiety, and Roger grinned at her; but that didn't greatly help.

"Roger, you look ghastly!"

"Tired, that's all."

"What's happened to your chin?"

"Had a row with a bad man," said Roger, "and it's all right, darling; he's in jail. Looks as if the job's working out, too. All I need is a good night's rest, preceded by a potent whisky-and-soda. Come to think," he added, hugging her, "I wouldn't mind a snack, either, I haven't had anything to eat since tea." He closed the door behind him. "The boys all right?"

"I think they had a funny kind of day at school," Janet said. "Half heroes, and half suspect because of the way the *Witness* talked about you. Scoopy had two fights, and Richard one."

Roger chuckled.

"Pity they can't stand in for me in the morning! I'm booked for the carpet, sweet, at ten o'clock sharp. Then I'll find out what kind of a bird Jay really is."

"You don't seem very worried."

"If he suspends me for a month, it'll be all holiday," Roger said, "and I don't see that he can do much more. In fact I don't think he can suspend me, after what's turned up, unless he's going to do it on the principle of asserting and maintaining authority. If he does it could be damned awkward, I wasn't exactly the model of discipline."

"You get your drink," Janet said; "I'll go and cook some bacon and eggs." She didn't add that it was easy to see that Roger was much more worried than he made out.

It was also easy to tell the difference in temper and temperature at the Yard. The men who had been wary and aloof, sitting on the fence in case Roger ran into serious trouble, jumped down on his side. The evidence spoke loudly for him. Even the *Witness* justified him. No one said much about Jay, except Eddie Day and Carter, who were together in the office when Roger went in.

"Any idea how 'e'll jump, Handsome?" Eddie demanded, and when Roger shook his head, went on: "You got the results all right, lucky for you you did, but I've always warned you that this lone-wolf business will get you into trouble one of these days. Got to have discipline, and you can't expect every A.C. to be like Chatworth."

"Dry up, Eddie," said Carter. "Good luck, Handsome."

Roger said "Thanks," and left for the Assistant Commissioner almost at once.

He tapped, and entered Miss Foster's outer office. For once she jumped up, greeted him with a smile which was probably meant to be warm and friendly, and said: "The Colonel wants you to go straight in, Mr. West."

"Thanks." Roger nodded.

The Colonel was standing by the window, looking out on to the Embankment. Every time he saw him standing up, Roger realised afresh that he was quite short; a little martinet of a man who wouldn't have got into the Metropolitan Police Force had he been required to pass the usual height regulation. He looked rather elderly, too, perhaps a little tired.

No one else was in the office.

"Ah, West," he said, and turned to look at Roger up and down, and then gaze very straightly into his eyes. "I'm fresh from the Army, as you know, where different standards and different values prevail. Between ourselves, I want you to know that I strongly disapprove of some of the methods you adopt, and that I feel that certain disciplinary standards must be established and maintained. However, there are certain emotional factors to consider, and there is the practical factor – that we have solved this case before more harm was done, largely due to your efforts. In view of that, I propose to ask you to draw up a full report, as detailed as you can make it, and to pass this over to Superintendent Cortland. You will then prepare the case against all the accused, in association with the Superintendent and the Public Prosecutor's office, devoting all your time to the task. I imagine that the case will be up for hearing in about five weeks' time, when you will see it through court."

Jay paused.

Roger felt as if new blood had been pumped into his veins.

"I have been studying your record closely," Jay went on, as if eager to make sure that the relief wasn't too long-lived, "and I find that you have an accumulation of over eight weeks' leave due. At the conclusion of the case against the accused I want you to take that leave. At the end of it the circumstances may have changed. Perhaps both you and I will look on them differently from the way we do at the moment. You may make arrangements for the holiday whenever you wish."

Roger said: "Thank you, sir," and couldn't prevent warmth from creeping into his voice. For in a few months' time this case and its sensations and rumours would be practically forgotten; and when his leave started, it would be in the flush of success.

"I think that is all," finished Jay. "Let my secretary know any time you wish to see me."

"Very good," Roger said. "Good day, sir."

Jay nodded.

Outside his office, Roger wiped the sweat from his forehead again, blew out his breath and then walked towards the stairs. He began to quicken his pace. There was a load of work waiting on the desk, there were three hearings in the magistrates' courts, all waiting for him to give evidence, and it was going to take him all his time to get it done. Afterwards, two months' leave—

Janet would refuse to believe it.

When he reached the office, he was grinning; when he went inside, Eddie Day looked up, eagerly, saw his expression and allowed one of acute disappointment to spread over his face. Carter looked up and said: "You haven't got *him* eating out of your hand, too!"

"Judgement deferred until this job's over," Roger said briskly, and winked at Sloan, who was at his desk. "Any news from Hadworth hospital?"

"Yes," Sloan said. "Henry's still hanging on, but there isn't much hope he'll live. He's made a statement, and I shouldn't think you need another thing, Roger."

"Good. Quist out?"

"Yes – the nine o'clock court."

"Fine," said Roger, and sat down at his desk and pulled the files towards him.

JOHN CREASEY

GIDEON'S DAY

Gideon's day is a busy one. He balances family commitments with solving a series of seemingly unrelated crimes from which a plot nonetheless evolves and a mystery is solved.

One of the most senior officers within Scotland Yard, George Gideon's crime solving abilities are in the finest traditions of London's world famous police headquarters. His analytical brain and sense of fairness is respected by colleagues and villains alike.

'The finest of all Scotland Yard series' – New York Times.

GIDEON'S FIRE

Commander George Gideon of Scotland Yard has to deal successively with news of a mass murderer, a depraved maniac, and the deaths of a family in an arson attack on an old building south of the river. This leaves little time for the crisis developing at home ....

'Gideon of Scotland Yard emerges as one of the most real working detectives in modern fiction.... A sympathetic and believable professional policeman.' - New York Times

JOHN CREASEY

THE CREEPERS

"The prisoner's hand was thin and bony ... And in the centre of the palm was a pinkish mark. It was the shape of a wolf's head, mouth open, fangs showing. Although it was what he had expected to see, Inspector West felt a twinge of repugnance a stab not unrelated to fear. It was the fifth time he had seen the mark of the wolf – the mark of Lobo."

A gang of cat burglars led by Lobo cause mayhem as they terrorize the city. They must be stopped, but with little in the way of evidence the police are baffled. Just how can Inspector West manage to do this in what is a race against time before more victims succumb?

"Here is an excellent novel of law enforcement officers, harried, discouraged and desperately fatigued, moving inexorably ahead under the pressure of knowledge that they must succeed to save human lives." - Cleveland Plain-Dealer

"Furiously exciting" - Chicago Tribune

"The action is fast, continuous and exciting" - San Francisco News

JOHN CREASEY

THE HOUSE OF THE BEARS

Standing alone in the bleak Yorkshire Moors is Sir Rufus Marne's 'House of the Bears'. Dr. Palfrey is asked to journey there to examine an invalid - who has now disappeared. Moreover, Marne's daughter lies terribly injured after a fall from the minstrel's gallery which Dr. Palfrey discovers was no accident. He sets out to investigate and the results surprise even him . . . .

"'Palfrey' and his boys deserve to take their places among the immortals." - Western Mail

INTRODUCING THE TOFF

Whilst returning home from a cricket match at his father's country home, the Honourable Richard Rollison - alias The Toff - comes across an accident which proves to be a mystery. As he delves deeper into the matter with his usual perseverance and thoroughness, murder and suspense form the backdrop to a fast moving and exciting adventure.

'The Toff has been promoted to a place of honour among amateur detectives.' – The Times Literary Supplement

Printed in Great Britain
by Amazon